Campfire Girls' Trip up the River

How Ethel Hollister
Became a Campfire Girl

By
IRENE ELLIOTT BENSON

Chicago
M. A. DONOHUE & COMPANY

CANOE AND CAMPFIRE SERIES

Four Books of Woodcraft and Adventure in the Forest and on the Water that every Boy Scout should have in his Library

By ST. GEORGE RATHBORNE

CANOEMATES IN CANADA; or, Three Boys Afloat on the Saskatchewan.
THE YOUNG FUR-TAKERS; or, Traps and Trails in the Wilderness.
THE HOUSE-BOAT BOYS; or, Drifting Down to the Sunny South.
CHUMS IN DIXIE; or, The Strange Cruise of a Motor Boat.
CAMP MATES IN MICHIGAN; or, With Pack and Paddle in the Pine Woods.
ROCKY MOUNTAIN BOYS; or, Camping in the Big Game Country.

In these four delightful volumes the author has drawn bountifully from his thirty-five years experience as a true sportsman and lover of nature, to reveal many of the secrets of the woods, such as all Boys Scouts strive to know. And, besides, each book is replete with stirring adventures among the four-footed denizens of the wilderness; so that a feast of useful knowledge is served up, with just that class of stirring incidents so eagerly welcomed by all boys with red blood in their veins. For sale wherever books are sold, or sent prepaid for 50 cents each by the publishers.

CONTENTS

CAMPFIRE GIRLS SERIES

HOW ETHEL HOLLISTER BECAME A
CAMPFIRE GIRL

ETHEL HOLLISTER'S SECOND SUMMER
AS A CAMPFIRE GIRL

CAMPFIRE GIRLS MOUNTAINEERING

CAMPFIRE GIRL'S RURAL RETREAT

CAMPFIRE GIRLS IN THE FOREST

CAMPFIRE GIRL'S LAKE CAMP

List Price 75c Each

How Ethel Hollister Became A Camp Fire Girl

CHAPTER I

A FASHIONABLE MOTHER

"No indeed, Kate!" ejaculated Mrs. Hollister emphatically, "Ethel has no time to join any Camp Fire Girls or Girl Scout Societies. She has her home and school duties, while her leisure is fully occupied. At present I know with whom she associates. As I understand it, these girls form themselves into a Company with a Guardian or Leader. They wear certain uniforms with emblems on the waists and sleeves, as well as a ring and bands of beads on their heads, all of which savors of conspicuousness, and it seems to me ridiculous."

"But, Aunt Bella," replied her niece, "think of what it makes of these girls. It teaches them to take care of themselves.

They very often sleep out of doors for two
months and get an honor for it."

"Yes, imagine a delicate girl like Ethel
doing that," rejoined Mrs. Hollister. "Why,
she'd contract pneumonia or consumption
right away."

"But if she were delicate she wouldn't
be allowed to do so unless by the advice of
a physician. Then for one month she's
obliged to give up sodas and candies between meals."

"Yes, and isn't that silly? Why, any
girl can do that without belonging to a
society."

"Well, they become healthy and strong;
they play all kinds of out of door athletic
games; they swim, dive, undress in deep
water, paddle or row twenty miles in any
five days; they learn to sail all kinds of
boats for fifty miles during the summer,
ride horse back, bicycle, skate, climb mountains, and even learn how to operate an
automobile."

"There, Kate, stop; you make me ner-
vous. Now what good is all such exercise
to a girl?"

"Why, it gives her the splendid health so necessary to every woman, and oh! if only you'd read about it. You won't listen, but they learn how to cook, how to market, to wash and iron, and keep house, how to take care of babies,—and don't you see if a girl marries a poor man she can be a help to him and not a hindrance?" Then they have to be kind and courteous, to look for and find the beauties of Nature until work becomes a pleasure and they're happy, cheerful and trustworthy. They give their services to others and learn something new all the time."

"My dear Kate," said her aunt, "nowadays a girl has all she can possibly do to fit herself for her future position in society; that is, if her family amounts to anything socially. Why should a girl learn to cook and market unless she intends to marry a poor man, and I don't propose that Ethel shall ever do that. And as for being so athletic, I don't approve of that either. It's all right for a girl to ride. Ethel is a good horsewoman; she learned from a splendid riding master. She plays tennis,

golf, and can swim; so you see she has
nearly all the requirements of Camp Fire
Girls."

"Oh, Aunt Bella, she has hardly any.
Why, look at the Boy Scout movement—
how marvellous it is and how it has grown.
It has become an institution, and in England when several Boy Scouts while camping
out were drowned, the Government (think
of it) sent out a gunboat—sent it up the
Thames to bring their bodies back to Lon-
don. Think of the National recognition.
Why, it's spreading so that every boy will
become a Scout before long. And the
good that they do no one knows."

"Well, my dear," said the elder lady,
"you are an enthusiast, and naturally
as you are a "Captain" or "Guardian," as
they call it, your sympathies are all with
the organization. But to me it's like
marching with the suffragettes. It belongs
to the women who favor "Woman's Rights,"
but not for a girl like Ethel."

"But you certainly approve of the
"Scout" movement, don't you? Why,
boys are joining from every rank of life."

"Ah! my dear," broke in Mrs. Hollister, "that's the great trouble. They *are* from every rank, and that's why I object. Had I a son I should not care to have him become interested in it, and for a girl like Ethel to rub shoulders with 'Tom, Dick and Harry,' it's simply not to be thought of. No, when she marries I trust it will be to a man who can afford to give her enough servants to do the work, a chauffeur to run her automobile, and a captain to sail her yacht. I hope she'll have a competent cook to bake her breads and prepare the soups, roasts, salads, and make preserves. I should feel very badly if she had to wash and iron, wipe her floors, or do any menial work. Were such a thing to happen, I hope I shall not live to see it, that's all. No, kindly drop the subject. Ethel is but sixteen. She'll have all she can do to finish at Madame La Rue's by the time she's eighteen. You know how hard your Uncle Archie works to obtain the money to pay for Ethel's education, and how I manage to keep up appearances on so little. It's all for Ethel. It means everything for her future. She must have the best associates, and when she graduates go with the fashionable set. We are very poor and she must marry well and have her own establishment. All of this Camp Girl business would be of no earthly benefit to her. It's only a fad and I believe not only that, but the "Scout" movement will die a natural death after a while. Young people must have some way to work off their superfluous energy; these Societies help them to do so. Now remember, Kate, you have a fairly well-to-do father and you need not worry over your future. Not so poor Ethel. That I have to look out for. *Please do not refer to this subject again, especially before her. I mean it and shall resent it if you do. I'm sure you'll respect my wishes in the matter."

"Of course, I shall, Aunt Bella," replied Kate, "but were you to more thoroughly understand this new movement I'm sure you'd view it differently and change your mind. The Boy Scouts have done so much good, and now this Camp Fire Girl is going to be such an improvement over the ordinary

girl. She's going to revolutionize young
women and make of them useful members
of society—not frivolous butterflies—and
it will be carried into the poorer classes and
teach girls who have never had a chance,
so that they may become good cooks and
housekeepers and love beautiful things.
And their costume is so pretty and sensible.
Oh! I wish you could see it with my eyes."

"To me, my dear, it is very like the Salvation Army. They wear badges and uniforms, and they too do much good, I am
told. Yet I shouldn't care to have my
Ethel become a member of that organization. But hush—remember your promise—
not a word. Here she comes."

CHAPTER II

ETHEL HOLLISTER

A young girl entered. She was lovely with the beauty of a newly opened rose. Her features were exquisite. Her rippling brown hair matched her eyes in color. Her complexion was creamy white with a faint touch of pink in either cheek. Although her figure was girlish it was perfectly formed and she carried herself well; still she looked delicate.

The mother and daughter were alike save where Mrs. Hollister's face was hard and worldly, Ethel's was soft and innocent.

"Well, dearie," said her mother, "here's an invitation for you from the Kips. Dorothy will celebrate her fifteenth birthday on Saturday with a luncheon and matinee party."

"Oh, how perfectly lovely," exclaimed the girl, showing her pretty teeth as she laughed. "Dorothy is such a dear. Why,

she hardly knows me. She's only been at
Madam's half a term."

"Never under-rate yourself, Ethel,"
spoke up Mrs. Hollister. "Remember that
you belong to one of New York's oldest
families. Although you have but little
money, people are sure to seek you not only
for your family name but because you are
an acquisition to any society."

Ethel blushed painfully while Cousin
Kate gazed out upon the budding
leaves on a tree in front of the Hollister
house. By a keen observer her private
opinion might be read in every line of her
face. She loved Ethel and her grandmother
—old Mrs. Hollister. She pitied her Uncle
Archie, but she despised her Aunt Bella
and rejoiced that at least none of that lady's
blood flowed in her veins. She worried over
Ethel who, notwithstanding her mother's
worldliness was as yet unspoiled, for the
child inherited much of her father's good
sense. Still under the constant influence
of a woman of Mrs. Hollister's type it would
be strange if the daughter failed to follow
in some of her mother's footsteps or to im-
bibe some of her fallacies.

"I'm going up to tell Grandmama," said Ethel, and bursting into the room she kissed the old lady.

"Listen, Grandmama, I'm invited to Dorothy Kip's birthday—a luncheon and matinee party."

"That's lovely, my darling," replied the elderly woman. "When does it come off?"

"Next Saturday, and I presume we'll go to Sherry's to lunch. Think of it! I've never been there—I'm so glad," and she danced around the room. "And my new grey broadcloth suit with silver fox will be just right to wear. You know the lovely grey chiffon waist over Irish lace that Mamma has just finished, and my grey velvet hat with rosebuds and silver fox fur —won't it be stunning?"

"You'll look lovely, I know. But where is Cousin Kate?"

"Oh, she's with Mamma. I entered the room while they were in the midst of an argument and they stopped suddenly. I guess it was about me. You know how set Mamma is in her way, and she was reading the riot act about something. —As

Kate leaves here tomorrow, shouldn't you think that Mamma would be too polite to differ with her? But no, she was talking quite loudly. I wish I might go home with Kate. I'd like to see her father and mother; they must be lovely.

"They are," replied Grandmother Hollister. "Your Uncle John is my oldest boy, and he has the sunniest nature imaginable."

"Yes, and Kate does something in the world," replied the girl. "I wish I might belong to her Camp Fire Girls that she has told you and me about. But Mamma— why! I shouldn't even dare suggest it; in fact, she doesn't dream that I know about Kate's being the Guardian of a Company. I feared that she might be rude if I spoke of it and might say something to offend Kate. Well, good-bye dear, I just wanted to tell you," and with another kiss Ethel left the room.

CHAPTER III

GRANDMOTHER HOLLISTER

Old Mrs. Hollister's room was on the third floor back. It was large and sunny, but considering that she owned the house it was rather peculiar that she had such an inferior room. She and her sister Susan were the only children of Josiah Carpenter, a wealthy man living in Akron, Ohio. Upon his death the girls found themselves alone and heiresses. Alice, while visiting in New York, met Archibald Hollister, who belonged to an old and respected family but who was of no earthly account as a business man. His handsome face won pretty Alice Carpenter. He was not long in spending nearly all of her fortune, but he really was considerate enough to contract pneumonia and die before he obtained possession of her house, which fortunately was in her name and unmortgaged.

She had two sons—John, Kate's father,

who lived in Columbus, Ohio, and Archibald with whom she now made her home. Archibald loved his mother and begged her to let him pay her rent for the house, but she replied that if he would pay the taxes and keep the house in repair it would equal the rent.

Her sister Susan still lived in the same town where they had been born. She had never married. People told Archibald Hollister that his Aunt Susan was a millionaire. Every investment that she made was successful. She had adopted and educated two orphan boys, one of whom had died, while the other was finishing college, after which he was to become a lawyer. Aunt Susan seldom wrote of herself. She corresponded with Alice (Grandmother Hollister) about twice a year, and at Christmas she invariably sent her a generous check.

Grandmother Hollister and her son were alike in many ways. They were free from all false pride and privately they considered Mrs. Hollister a snob, and worried lest Ethel should become one. Archibald seldom asserted himself, but when he did

his word was law. While his wife was a
social climber he was exactly the opposite.
He had been known to bring home the most
disreputable looking men—men who had
been his friends in youth and who were
playing in hard luck. He would ask them
to dinner without even sending word, and
his wife would invariably plead a sick
headache to get rid of sitting with them.
She dared not interfere nor object for she
was just a little afraid of him and she
realized that in nearly everything he allowed her to have her own way.

Mrs. Hollister told Ethel privately that
both here father and grandmother were old
fashioned. Although living in a handsome
house they kept but one maid. Mr. Hollister's salary was but a little over three
thousand, and at times they had hard
work to make both ends meet. Ethel
attended a fashionable school and hardly
realized what the family sacrificed for her.
She made many friends among the wealthy
girls of the smart set. Thanks to her
mother's skill and taste she was enabled to
dress beautifully, but youth is thoughtless

and she was just a little too self centered to
see that her parents were depriving themselves for her.

Mrs. Hollister gave bridge parties, and
once every two weeks a tea for Ethel. Upon
those days she hired two extra maids. It
was pitiable to see how she strove to keep
up appearances. There was a young man
whose sister went with the set of girls who
came to Ethel's teas. His name was Harvey
Bigelow. One of his sisters had married
into the nobility. He had a large Roman
nose and a receding forehead, but Mrs.
Hollister was delighted when one afternoon
Nannie Bigelow—his sister—brought him
to the house. He was only nineteen and at
college. Ethel disliked him from the first.

"Why, dear, why are you so rude to
Mr. Bigelow? He's a gentleman," said
Mrs. Hollister.

"Yes, Mamma, but I simply cannot
endure him," replied the girl. "For one
thing his nails are too shiny, and that shows
his lack of refinement. I don't care if his
sister married the King, he's common—
that's all."

It was then that Mrs. Hollister would declare that Ethel was exactly like her father and grandmother.

CHAPTER IV

A PINK TEA

Although old Mrs. Hollister owned the house and nearly all of the handsome antique furniture, Mrs. Archie seemed often to forget that fact, and from her manner one might infer that the lady regarded her mother-in-law as a sort of interloper. The old lady would allow her to go just so far, after which she would suddenly pull her up with a sharp turn and admonish her with such a cutting rebuke that Mrs. Archie would blush painfully and apologize. But while antagonistic on most points they each agreed on Ethel. Even Grandmother felt that her daughter-in-law was wise in trying to fit the girl for the smart set, where she would have social position and money, and she even sided with the wife against her son, who considered it all wrong.

One afternoon Archibald Hollister came home early and ran right into the "Pink

Tea" crowd. Old Mrs. Hollister, tastefully gowned in black and white, sat in the
library where the maids brought up refreshments to her. A young musician whose
mother had been a schoolmate of Mrs.
Hollister's, and who was poor, played the
piano from four to seven for the small sum
of three dollars. Everything went off pleas-
antly. The maids acted as though they
were really fixtures in the house. The
refreshments were excellent. No wonder
with the line of autos before the door
people considered the Hollisters wealthy,
"but plain and solid with no airs, etc."

Old Mrs. Hollister enjoyed young people's
society, and they all voted her a dear.
She'd invite their confidences, and before
leaving each girl would come up to the
library for a chat with Grandmother.

"Oh, Mrs. Hollister," said Lottie Owen,
a girl of Ethel's age, "have you heard about
the 'turkey trot?' We can't dance it any
more,—it's been suppressed."

"How does it go?" asked the old lady.
"I've read something of it."

"Well, just wait,—I'll get Nannie Bigelow and we'll dance it for you."

Thereupon the two girls would show Grandmother Hollister the steps.

"That's something like the 'Boston Dip,'" responded she very much excited. "Why, when I was a girl my mother took me away from a cotillion one night because they danced it," and she grew pretty as she excitedly told of her younger days.

"I bet you were lovely, Mrs. Hollister," said Nannie. "Ethel will never be as pretty as you were. We were looking at your portrait in the drawing room. You must have been fascinating, and as for Mr. Hollister—your husband—well, he was just a dear."

The old lady blushed. Here Lottie spoke up:

"Yes, and people say you were such a belle. Old Mr. Tupper was at our house and met Ethel, and he told us a lot about you. But here's Mr. Hollister," and they rushed forward to greet her son.

"Well, well!" he exclaimed gallantly, "I didn't expect to get into such a garden of roses. And you, too, Mother—why, you've actually grown younger."

"That's just what we tell her," said Nannie. "We've been dancing the 'turkey trot' for her," they whispered, slyly kissing her goodbye.

These were happy afternoons for Grandmother, after which she and her son would sit and chat.

"It sort of livens things up to have young people about, doesn't it, Mother?" he said, taking a cup of tea and a sandwich.

"Yes, Archid, it certainly does; but you look tired."

"I am, Mother," replied the man. "I wish Ethel was finished with her school and happily married. This strain is telling on me and I suppose poor Bella suffers from it even as I do."

"It's too bad, Archie. I don't like this sailing under false colors. People imagine Ethel a wealthy girl. Probably they think she'll inherit my money. Of course, they never dream that I'm penniless and that you have a salary of only three thousand a year; but so long as we keep out of debt I don't know as we are doing wrong."

"Has Kate gone?" he asked.

"Yes, she left this morning. Bella took her to the train. She's gone to visit her mother's people in Tarrytown. Kate's a nice girl."

"She's a sensible girl. I only hope that Ethel will grow into as good a woman as Kate Hollister," said Archibald.

"You see, Kate has a new fad," began Grandmother—"not a fad either; its purpose is too earnest to call it that. She is the head of a Company of girls called "Camp Fire Girls." They are something like the "Boy Scout Organization." The object is to make girls healthy. It gives them knowledge; it causes them to work and learn to love it; it makes them trustworthy; they begin to search for beauty in Nature and they're perfectly happy. I remember that much, but the sum and substance of it is that it teaches a girl everything that is useful. Kate is the Guardian of one Camp Fire section. They meet weekly and from what she tells me it must be a great thing. Kate spoke of it to Bella but she ridiculed it and forbade her to speak of it to Ethel. She declares it is like the

Salvation Army, etc., and Kate promised
not to, I think she had hoped to secure
Ethel for one of the girls next summer."

"Well, there's no need of us trying to
oppose Bella," said her son. "She is
determined that Ethel shall make a brilliant
match and in her eyes this would be a waste
of time. No, Mother, the best thing for
you and me to do is to travel along the lines
of the least resistance. Come,—dinner is
ready. I'll help you down."

CHAPTER V

AN INVITATION TO AUNT SUSAN

One afternoon Mrs. Hollister called Ethel into her room. After closing the door she said, "Ethel, I have written to your father's Aunt Susan, who lives in Akron, to come here and make us a visit. You know she's Grandmother's only sister, and I think it will do them both good to see each other. Grandmother is delighted and I expect that Aunt Susan will accept," and Mrs. Hollister calmly drew on her gloves.

Now, as her mother was not in the habit of considering her grandmother's comfort, and as the two women were seldom of one accord, Ethel looked at her furtively and with a puzzled expression of countenance, but that lady acted not the least embarrassed. It seemed strange to Ethel that all at once she should wish to cheer up her mother-in-law by inviting her country sister to visit them, but the girl simply said:

"That's lovely, Mamma," and went up
to her room to study.

Although she disliked to credit her mother
with such artifices, she finally hit upon a
solution of the object of the invitation. It
must be that it was Aunt Susan's money
she was after, and why? Suddenly, it all
came to the girl—it was to get Aunt Susan
to like her (Ethel, her grand-niece) and
make her her heiress, if not to all at least to
a part of her fortune.

Ethel sat and gazed at the pretty room in
which Mrs. Hollister had spent so much
time decorating and making attractive.
In her heart there was a desire to denounce
her mother. Then, when she realized that
it was all being done to benefit herself, she
could feel nothing but pity for the woman
whose one thought in life was for her daughter. She thought: "She will even tell
people that I am Aunt Susan's heiress, and
I must sit by and know that it is untrue.
Everything is untrue in this house. Oh,
how I wish I could get away from it all!"
But to her grandmother she told her sus-
picions.

"Never mind, my lamb," said the old lady. "I know Susan well enough to say that she will love you for yourself, and probably she does intend to leave you and Kate half of her fortune at least. If it serves to help your mother socially, why Susan wouldn't care—she'd only laugh. Susan's very keen and sharp, my child. No one can make her do what she doesn't care to. Now don't you worry over anything. When she comes just be kind and polite to her and help make her visit pleasant."

"But, Grandmama, I should die of mortification if she even conceived the idea that mother had that in her mind when she asked her here for a visit. Oh, I couldn't endure it. Please never let her know what I suspect. Will you promise, or I cannot look into her face."

"Your Aunt Susan shall never suspect such a thing from me. I promise," replied Grandmama Hollister. "I am only too glad to see her once more. I could almost forgive your mother for any duplicity in it so long as she can come, for Susan and I are growing old and it will not be many years before one of us goes. But, Ethel, don't expect to see any style. Aunt Susan is a plain country woman. It may be a trial for you to have to go out with her."

"Oh, never, if she's like you, Grandmother," said the girl, kissing her, "and she is your own sister. She must be like you. But there's Nannie Bigelow and Grace McAllister. I wonder what they want."

"Hello! Ethel," called two young voices, "we're coming up. Your mother said we might."

"All right, girls; I'm in Grandmamma's room," replied Ethel, "come in here."

After greeting the old lady affectionately they began: "What do you know about it?" said Grace—"here Dorothy Kip has joined a new Society called the "Camp Fire Girls," and from the first day of vacation— May fifteenth—until October she's going to live in the woods and camp out."

"Yes," broke in Nannie Bigelow, "I'm just crazy to belong but Mamma won't let me because she heard that two of the girls who are to be in the Company live in the Bronx in a small flat and go to public school.

But Connie Westcott's aunt is to be the head or 'Guardian,' and these girls are in her Sunday School class. She likes them and insists upon their becoming members. Isn't it ridiculous, Mrs. Hollister, that just because these girls are poor they're not considered fit to associate with us by some mothers, and I mean mine. As if I was half as good as they. Why, my great-grandfather was a shoemaker. Papa told me all about it, and he was a dandy good shoemaker, too; but Mother gets furious when I refer to it," and Nannie threw herself in a chair before the open fire that Grandmother Hollister always kept lighted save in warm weather.

"I know my mother wouldn't let me join," said Ethel. "Why, Kate Hollister is the Guardian of a Company in Columbus, Ohio, and Mother wouldn't allow her to speak of it even. She says it's like the Salvation Army, and such ridiculous nonsense. Oh, dear! all the mothers are alike, I'm afraid. We'll never have real fun until after we're married or become old maids."

Just then they were interrupted by the arrival of Connie Westcott, Dorothy Kip, and two or three more of Ethel's young friends, to whom they explained the subject under discussion.

"Well, my mother will let me join," said Connie, "and Dorothy's has allowed her."

"Yes," broke in Dorothy, "I was sure Mother would allow me to if Miss Westcott was to be the Guardian."

"It must be a fine organization," said Mrs. Hollister, knitting steadily with the yellow lace falling over her still pretty hands. "I wish we had known of something like that in my young day. Why, it must be like one continuous picnic."

"I'll tell you what they do," said Sara Judson, "they first learn how to put out a fire. Supposing one's clothes should catch; they could save one's life. Then, in summer, or through the ice in winter, they rescue drowning people who have never learned to swim. They know what to do for an open cut; for fainting; how to bandage and use surgeon's plaster. They can cook at least two meals, mend stockings,

sew, etc., and keep one's self free from colds
and illness. They sleep in the open, and
my! what fine health it gives a girl, and it
makes a perfect athlete of her. She can
cook and bake, market, and know just how
to choose meats and vegetables. She can
become a fine housekeeper as well, and learn
how to make lovely gardens. Why, I'll
bring you a book, Mrs. Hollister. I could-
n't begin to tell you how wonderful it is.
If a girl lives up to all the rules and can
learn everything that is taught she's a
wonder, that's all. So I hope some day
Ethel can join, even if later."

"Oh, I'll never be allowed to join, girls.
I'm to be a parlor ornament," and Ethel's
eyes filled with tears.

"Never mind," said Constance White,
"how desolate the home furnishings would
be without lovely bric-a-brac."

"Yes," replied Grandmother Hollister,
"whatever position a girl occupies if she
fills it creditably she will have done her
duty."

"I know that Ethel will be the head of a
large and magnificent establishment," said

Nannie Bigelow. "She's just the style of a girl."

Ethel half laughed and dried her eyes on her Grandmother's handkerchief.

"I don't care," she faltered, "think of living out in a camp and sitting around the fire telling stories. And I shall never be allowed to do it."

"Now you buck up, old girl," said Dorothy Kip abruptly. "Oh, excuse me, Mrs. Hollister, but sometimes I just love to use slang. You go ahead and wish hard for what you want and you'll get it. I always do. Say, don't you know that you can influence others to think exactly as you do? By wishing with all your might you can will it to be done."

Everyone laughed. Dorothy was an odd roly poly pretty girl of fifteen. She was the only sister and idol of four brothers whom she copied in every way. The newest slang was invariably on her tongue, and the family laughed at and petted her. In their eyes everything she did was perfect. She was a general favorite at school, but Madam La Rue declared that she would never become a perfect lady while her brothers lived at home; but she was kind-hearted and generous. Mrs. Hollister, Senior, liked her immensely. She always called her "Grandma."

"Do you know what I'm going in for?" she asked of the old lady. "Well, I'll tell you—it's babies!" Everyone laughed.

"You needn't laugh. Next year I'm going to take all of my spending money excepting ten dollars and hire two rooms and a kitchenette. Dad gives me sixty dollars per. I'm going to take thirty-five for rent and the boys will help me furnish. Then I'm going to beg my friends for contributions and open a Day Nursery. Of course, I'll have to get a woman for fifteen dollars a month to take care of the babies, and the mothers can pay four cents a day for each child."

"Why, Dorothy Kip," exclaimed the girls. "You couldn't get any servant for fifteen dollars a month."

"I can, and don't you forget it. Old Susan Conner, who used to be my brother Tom's nurse, has offered to come for fif-

teen dollars.   She likes me and she's willing
to help me in this charity.   "We've talked
it all over.   Susan is some class now and
has her two-room-and-bath apartment.
She's old and hasn't much to do and she
has enough to live on, so she's offered to
come; and I'm going to spend just ten
dollars on myself each month in place of
sixty for candy and soda and such nonsense.
No one knows of it but Susan and I.   I'm
going to beg for oatmeal and rice and bread
of the grocers with whom we've traded
for years, and if they refuse I'll influence
Mother to leave them.   Then I think Dad
will help me out on milk and anything
needed.   I'll confide in him."

"That's a fine and magnificent idea,
Dorothy," said Mrs. Hollister, "and you'll
become a public benefactor."

"Well, you see, Mrs. Hollister, I like the
little kids and I've seen such pitiful faces
on some where the sisters have had to take
care of them while the mothers worked.
So I made up my mind I could take ten
little ones anyway.   Then the mothers'
four cents will be forty cents a day.   That

will pay for some of the food. Oh! I'm
going to become a beggar and ask every
friend to help me. Maybe it will fail but
I can try. The boys will give, I'm sure."

"Yes, Dorothy, and I bet you'll suc-
ceed," said the girls. "We'll help, too."

Then each girl pledged herself for what
she could afford to give.

"Well, you're awfully good, I'm sure,"
said Dorothy. "I never dreamed you'd
all come forward. You're certainly sports,
every one of you, and I'm obliged more
than I can tell you."

"Who knows," said Grandmother Hollister, "but when you're grown up, you'll
have a large house, and it may be called
'The Kip Day Nursery' and each of you
girls here may be lady managers. They
all grow from small beginnings. And, Dorothy, you may put me down for ten dollars,"
said Mrs. Hollister.

"Oh, say, you're a thoroughbred, you
are," and the girl kissed her impulsively
several times.

Now Grandmother Hollister had been
saving that particular ten for a new lace

scarf. It had been sent to her on her birthday by her son John, but she couldn't resist
giving it. She could do without the scarf,
and ten dollars would buy a couple or more
warm rugs for the babies to sit on, for little
ones like to sit on the floor.

The girls stayed in her room and chatted
until dusk. They talked as freely before
the old lady as before one another.

That evening Ethel asked her grandmother if there wasn't some way by which
she could get away that summer and go to
visit Cousin Kate.

"I'll think it over," replied Grandmother; "you certainly need the country.
You look thin and peaked."

"Yes, and Mamma will take me to New-
port or Narragansett, and I hate it. Why,
it's just like New York. You meet the very
same people and I never cared for the water
as I care for inland or mountains. Do
think out a way, Grandmamma. You
always manage to do everything just right."

"I'll try," replied Mrs. Hollister.

CHAPTER VI

The next morning there came a letter of acceptance from Aunt Susan. She would arrive on Friday. This was Thursday. Grandmother Hollister hummed a little song as she went up stairs.

"It will do Mother lots of good," ejaculated Mr. Hollister. "It was kind of you, Bella, to think of that."

Mrs. Hollister blushed. Ethel watched her as she slowly sipped her coffee. Mrs. Hollister was a peculiar woman. She was truthful and frank when she wished to be. Now she realized that her husband trusted and had faith in her and that Ethel was furtively watching her, so she said: "Well, Archie, perhaps I was a little selfish in asking Aunt Susan. Perhaps I did it to help Ethel a bit as well as to please Mother. Aunt Susan is wealthy. Now why shouldn't Ethel come in for some of her money as well as that adopted boy?"

"Why, Bella," said her husband, "is it possible that you had only that idea in your head when you invited my aunt here?"

"No, not entirely. I knew that it would please your mother, and I could kill two birds with one stone. That's why."

Ethel saw a peculiar look come upon her father's face. She had noticed it when he brought home his disreputable looking friends to dine and when her mother objected. He turned to his daughter.

"Ethel," he said, "I wish you to help and make your Aunt Susan's visit very pleasant. I would like you to take her out and show her everything, and Grandmother must go along also. You will be doing me a great favor if you will."

"Papa, I'll do my best to make it pleasant," replied the girl, kissing him.

Then, without looking at his wife, Mr. Hollister left the room, followed by his daughter.

"So that was her object!" he exclaimed, as Ethel helped him on with his coat. "What would Aunt Susan think were she to know? Your mother wishes you to ingratiate yourself with my aunt so that she'll leave you the lion's share of her money. Why, she'd probably leave my brother John and me a remembrance anyway, and you and Kate would benefit by it. Well, this is a strange world, my child. I wish your mother was less politic, but I presume it is done for you, Ethel, so we mustn't be too hard on her. She's a good mother to you, my dear, and has great ambition for you. I only hope that you'll be happy. Never marry for money alone— that's a sin—remember."

"I will, Papa," said the girl blushing. "I may never marry, and then you and I can live together. Wouldn't we have fun?"

Aunt Susan arrived. Ethel gazed at her spellbound. She had the kindest face she had ever seen, but oh! how old fashioned she looked. Her grey hair was drawn tightly back into a cracker knot. In front she wore a bunch of tight frizzes under a little flat velvet hat with strings, something of the style of 1879. Her gown was of black made with a full skirt trimmed with black satin bands. She wore an old-fash-

ioned plush dolman heavily beaded and
covered with fringe. Her shoes were thick
like a man's, and to crown all she carried
a fish-net bag. She didn't seem to realize
that she looked behind the times.

Ethel thought that her teeth and eyes
were the loveliest that she had ever seen
on a woman of her age, for she was grandmother's senior. She and Mrs. Hollister
looked enough alike to be twins. They
fell upon each other's neck and wept.
Ethel was mentally hoping that Aunt Susan
would purchase some modern clothes or that
none of her fashionable friends would meet
her, for among them were some who would
laugh at the old lady, and the girl felt that
she'd die of mortification and anger,—not
the girls with whom she was intimate and
who came to see her daily, but the girls
who belonged to the exclusive set, and with
whom Ethel and her friends seldom went as
they were much younger.

The day following Mrs. Hollister phoned
for a taxi, and to Ethel's horror she ordered
an open one. Ethel was to take Aunt
Susan and Grandmother for a drive. She

dared not demur. Had she not promised
her father to do everything for Aunt Susan?
Could she hurt her dear grandmother's
feelings? And last of all, she would not
admit to her mother the fact that she was
ashamed of Aunt Susan's appearance. No,
so she went.

As it was early in April and cool, upon
this occasion Aunt Susan wore ear tabs,
over which she tied a thick, green veil.
when it grew warmer in the sunshine she
removed the veil. They drove up River-
side to Grant's Tomb, where Aunt Susan
insisted upon getting out. Fortunately
Ethel encountered no one whom she knew,
but as they were driving up Lafayette
Boulevard they passed Estelle Mason, one
of her swell friends. The chills ran up and
down Ethel's spine, while she sat with her
lips compressed. The girl bowed and de-
liberately giggled. Even grandmother, who
looked lovely, grew red. But Aunt Susan
seemed not to notice it.

"I am a snob just like mother," thought
the girl. "I ought to be ashamed of myself. I'll never speak to Estelle again,

the rude upstart! They say she prides herself on her family, but I can't see that her good blood has made a lady of her," and into Ethel's eyes came tears.

"Ethel, my dear," said Aunt Susan, "you're looking badly. Your cheeks are flushed. Do you feel ill?"

"No, Aunt Susan," she replied. "I always grow red when riding in the wind."

Grandmother had seen it all and pitied the girl.

"Deafness comes early in the Carpenter family," persisted Aunt Susan. "Here, take this veil, dear, do, and tie it over your ears."

But Ethel declined, and to her joy the ride was soon over.

In the privacy of her room Grandmother Hollister confided to Ethel that really Aunt Susan ought to dress differently.

"I understand how you felt, dear," she continued, "when you met that rude Mason girl and she laughed, but there's bad blood there. I know all about her and her grandparents. My dear child, her grandmother used to be a waitress way out West where

her grandfather owned mines, and he
boarded at the house where she worked, fell
in love and married her. Probably there's
where she gets her rudeness."

"Why, Grandmother, how did you know
that?" asked Ethel.

"There's little I don't know about the
fine old New York families, my dear.
Remember I married into one and I heard
a great deal."

After that Ethel felt comforted.

CHAPTER VII

AUNT SUSAN MAKES FRIENDS

In less than a week Mrs. Hollister had circulated the report that Aunt Susan was an immensely wealthy but eccentric old maid, and that Ethel was to be her heiress. The report spread like wildfire. Then Mrs. Hollister took the girl and told her that she must begin and make herself invaluable to Aunt Susan, so that she alone would inherit her immense fortune.

"Of course," she said, "she'll leave your Cousin Kate some if it, but why should that adopted son get the lion's share? You might just as well have it."

Ethel had to go everywhere with Aunt Susan,—she who so disliked anything savoring of the conspicuous. She could hear the sneers and laughter of Estelle Mason's set of girls and could see their looks of amusement. At first she rebelled, but the dislike of offending her grandmother and fear of disobeying her mother made her meekly submit, and like a martyr she went.

Aunt Susan was such a lovely character that Ethel was ashamed of herself, for everything seemed to please her so, and she kept dwelling upon the fact that the family (especially Ethel) was so kind that she should never forget it. But although she bought expensive gifts for the three women, they dared not suggest her spending anything on herself. Something kept them from it and told them that she might become offended and leave the house.

Gradually the friends of the Hollisters' came and fell in love with Aunt Susan. She was such a lady and had such charming manners. Besides, knowing her to be a wealthy woman, they accepted her with her peculiar gowns, even inviting her to teas, etc. Never did an old lady have such a fine visit. Harvey Bigelow was most attentive to her, Aunt Susan declaring him to be a likely fellow, and wondering why her niece Kate didn't fancy him.

"She spoke often of Thomas Harper—her adopted son and protege. He was a fine lawyer and was devoted to her. She received letters from him twice a week, from which she read extracts. Mrs. Hollister declared that he was crafty and after Aunt Susan's money, and it seemed to worry her not a little. She even started in to insinuate as much to the lady, who gazed at her peculiarly until Grandmother took her alone one day and said: "If ever you expect to make Aunt Susan fond of Ethel you are going to work the wrong way. She's very sharp, and if you speak ill of Thomas Harper you'll show your hand—I warn you.

"She'll do as she chooses and you can't compel her to do otherwise. She's fond of Ethel now for herself. I warn you, Bella, not to let your greediness make Susan know you as you are. I'd like her to keep the good opinion of you that she has at present."

Mrs. Hollister knew that her mother-in-law spoke the truth and she said nothing, but left the room.

CHAPTER VIII

ETHEL IS INVITED TO VISIT

One morning in May, as the last days of Aunt Susan's visit were drawing to a close, she said to Mrs. Hollister: "Bella, Ethel tells me that her vacation begins next week. Now I've been thinking it over. The child doesn't look strong. She needs country air. I don't mean your fashionable places, but where she can live out of doors in a simple gown, play games, and take long walks, etc. Now you've given me such a pleasant time that I'm going to invite her to go home with me. I'll wait for her school to close and we can start from here Saturday."

Mrs. Hollister was overjoyed. Of all things that was what she had most desired and, too, it would save them much expense, for a summer's trip to a fashionable hotel made a large hole in Archibald Hollister's salary.

"Yes, indeed, Aunt Susan, she will be

simply delighted to go," replied the lady.
"I'll get her ready at once."

"She'll need nothing new," called out
Aunt Susan. "We're very plain people.
We live simply, and her gowns and hats will
seem like visions of Paris fashions to the
girls in our town. Then I shall ask Kate to
come for a visit as well. And, by the way,
Bella, come back; I wish to say something.
You know my niece Kate goes up into Camp
this summer with her girls. Now I should
like Ethel to go along. It is a great movement—this Camp Fire movement—and it
will do the child lots of good, for she strikes
me as very delicate."

Mrs. Hollister gasped.

"Yes," she replied, "Kate spoke to me
of it but I shouldn't care for Ethel to
join."

"Why not?" asked Aunt Susan. "It
certainly is the most creditable thing any
girl can join. It's a wonderful institution.
What objection can you have?" and she
looked at her niece tentatively.

Mrs. Hollister reviewed the situation as
she stood there. It would not do for her

to air her objections to Aunt Susan. She
was just a little afraid of that lady and
wished her to have a good opinion of her,
so she continued reluctantly: "Well, you
see, Aunt Susan, it is such a strenuous life,
and Ethel is not over robust. I'm almost
afraid it might do her more harm than
good."

"Nonsense, Bella," replied Aunt Susan,
"that's the most shallow objection you
could advance. I should deem it a personal
favor if you'll give your consent."

Now Mrs. Hollister dared not withhold
her consent, and yet she was angry. That
Ethel was at last to be entrapped into belonging to that detestable Organization was
what she had never dreamed could take
place. She was caught and trapped; there
was no help. Even though she gave her
consent, after Ethel came home in the fall
she could talk her out of it. So she said
with a of show amiability: "Since you
desire it, Aunt Susan, I'll consent, but I
don't approve of it at all, I must admit."

"Thank you," replied Aunt Susan. "I
think you'll feel differently when you see

Ethel upon her return home this fall. All of the girls in Akron are joining. They're crazy over it."

Mrs. Hollister replied that she was open to conviction and should be glad if Ethel derived any benefit from it.

"But what shall I buy for her to wear?" she asked.

"I will attend to her outfit," replied Aunt Susan. "It is not expensive."

CHAPTER IX

Ethel was overjoyed that permission had been obtained to allow her to become a Camp Fire Girl.

"Isn't Aunt Susan clever to have been able to have gotten Mother to change her mind?"

Grandmother smiled but said nothing, but when alone Mrs. Hollister said: "Ethel, remember that you are in line for Aunt Susan's money. Grandmother says she admires you and thinks that you have shown her great courtesy—says you've been kindness itself to her—so it has paid, hasn't it, dear? Now your visit will do the business, and you'll probably come in for the lion's share. Of course, you are only sixteen, but who knows what may happen? When you finish school you may become the Duchess of Everton's sister-in-law—think of it—and I alone shall be responsible."

"Oh, Mamma," replied Ethel, growing red, "you know I am only a young girl yet. Besides, I loathe Harvey Bigelow. He talks through his nose and is vulgar."

"Nonsense," replied her mother, "look at all of the young men of today, especially among the rich. Are they so very good looking?"

"Yes," replied Ethel, "I think Dorothy Kip has four fine looking brothers, and I know lots of good looking young men, but I can't endure Harvey Bigelow although I love Nannie."

"Well, Harvey averages well as to looks, and think of his position and family, and you a poor man's daughter. If you'll be guided by me, my dear, I'll put you above them all. Were your father to die what could you do? Should you like to be a saleswoman?"

Ethel was angry but she knew that her mother spoke wisely. She, too, loved money and position, as well perhaps as Mrs. Hollister, but she was not quite so worldly.

The Saturday arrived at last and they

started for Akron. Although Ethel felt
ashamed to admit it, owing to Aunt Susan's
conspicuous appearance, she dreaded the
train ordeal, but there was no help for it.
She did speak of it to her mother, who
calmly surveyed her daughter and replied:
"Ethel, I fear you are a snob."

The girl regarded her mother with astonishment, who without embarrassment
calmly continued: "Did you ever see me
act as though I was ashamed of your aunt?"

And as Ethel thought, she was forced to
admit that she never had, for Mrs. Hollister was a strange anomaly. Her snob-
bishness seemed to lie in the desire to rise
socially—to take her place with the best—
but she never had seemed to even take
exception to Aunt Susan's appearance; in
fact, she felt that people would consider it
the eccentricity of a wealthy woman. She
went with her everywhere and never was
ashamed, therefore her reproof to her daughter was sincere.

CHAPTER X

The journey was very pleasant. Ethel enjoyed it. Aunt Susan removed her hat and tied the objectionable green veil around her head. This didn't seem quite so out of place. As they talked Ethel noticed that Aunt Susan was wonderfully well informed on every subject. She was like an encyclopedia, and her conversation was most interesting.

As they were nearing their destination many of her townspeople passed through the train. They greeted her most heartily with: "Well, well, Mrs. Carpenter, we have missed you. Had a pleasant time?"

"How's my boy?" she asked of one man.

"My, but he's fine," rejoined the man,— "won a big case the other day. Haven't you heard about it? Sears, the automobile man—someone accused him of infringing on his patent, and he—Sears—sued him.

Tom won the suit. Everyone is congratulating him," etc.

Each person had some report of Tom. "They seem to love Aunt Susan," thought Ethel. "It only goes to show how much people think of money. Perhaps were she poor they wouldn't notice her." But wasn't her own mother a money-worshipper, and didn't she herself care for people who had it? "I suppose it's the way of the world," she thought.

The train slowed into the depot. A tall broad-shouldered athletic looking fellow entered the car and grasped Aunt Susan by the waist, and as he lifted her almost from the floor he kissed her affectionately saying: "Oh, my! but Aunt Susan I've missed you," and his voice rang manly and true.

Ethel liked his face. He had keen but pleasant grey eyes, a square jaw, large mouth and fine teeth. "But alas!" she thought, "how terribly he dresses, with his loosely tied black cravat, a slouch hat, low collar and wide trousers—like types of eccentric literary men seen on the stage and in pictures."

He was absolutely devoid of style, yet everyone seemed to look up to him and lots of pretty girls blushed unconsciously as he returned their bows. Aunt Susan must have spoken to everyone who passed. They all seemed to know her well.

As they drove up and alighted at the door of a small plain house she must have noticed a disappointed look in her niece's eyes, for she said: "Your Grandmother and I were born here, my dear. That large house on the hill once belonged to me, but I disposed of it and moved here. I love the associations. Although it is very primitive. I trust you may be happy in it while visiting under its roof."

And indeed it was primitive with its wooden shutters and piazza with a stone floor made of pieces of flagging. The rooms were low-ceilinged with windows of tiny panes, whose white muslin curtains were trimmed with ball fringe made by Aunt Susan. There were ingrain carpets on the floor and old-fashioned mahogany furniture—the real thing, not reproductions.

It was massive and handsome with ex-quisite hand carving.

Ethel's floor was covered with the old-fashioned rag carpeting and rugs to match. Vases of roses were on the bureau and stand, evidently put there by "Mr. Thomas" as she called him.

CHAPTER XI

THE NEXT DAY

She slept as she had never before slept and was awakened in the morning by the robins that sang in the white blossomed cherry trees. It was so lovely that she lay quite still to listen. Then she arose, but before dressing she gazed out of the window. They were over a mile from the town. The path up from the gate was bordered on either side by spring flowers. Immense trees hid the road from view but she could hear the toot of the motors in passing and it all seemed strange, for the house was over one hundred years old, and everything, even to the pump in the yard, was so old-fashioned.

Ethel looked sideways at the house on the hill in which Aunt Susan told her she had once lived. It was immense,—more like an Institution. Probably it had been sold and remodeled, and perhaps was something of the sort now, thought Ethel.

She dressed and went down stairs. Aunt Susan must have been up some time, for the house looked so clean, and the odor of roses was everywhere,—roses on the old-fashioned piano, on the mantel, and on the breakfast table.

Ethel ate heartily, everything tasted so good. Old Jane, the maid of all work, had been with her Aunt Susan ever since her father's death many years before, and she was a woman who cooked most deliciously. Ethel wondered why Aunt Susan kept but one maid, although she ceased to wonder at anything after Aunt Susan had finished breakfast.

"Tom lives in Akron at the hotel," said she. "He has many clients, some of whom can only consult him in the evening, and that's why he cannot stay here with me. But until I left for New York," she continued, "I had the village school teacher for company. You see, although this place belongs to Akron, there are many children who cannot journey back and forth to school, so we have a little schoolhouse near. The teacher usually boards with me, and with Jane in the kitchen I am well protected."

Ethel pondered. She had solved the mystery. Aunt Susan was a miser, of that there was no doubt. Imagine a woman of her immense wealth taking a boarder and living as she did. Ethel wondered if at night when everyone was sound asleep she counted her money as misers do; and perhaps it was on this very mahogany table that she emptied the bags before counting.

What they had to eat was of the best and she enjoyed the ham and eggs and freshly churned butter. After a while she started up stairs, but Aunt Susan was ahead of her.

"Oh, Auntie, I wanted to make my own bed."

"Well, dear, you may after today, if you will. Jane is pretty old to go up and down stairs."

The change was so complete that Ethel felt like a new girl.

"I don't care if she is a miser," she thought, "she's just lovely and so like Grandmother; and I'll have a happy time, I know."

CHAPTER XII

ETHEL LEARNS TO COOK

Here is a page from her letter to her grandmother:

"Oh! my dear Grandmamma, you don't know how happy I am—not being away from those I love, but things are so different. I get up early and after breakfast I help Aunt Susan with the housework, for her maid is too old to go up and down stairs. I have learned to churn—to make butter and pot cheese as well. I dust, make my bed, and sweep my room. (Don't let mother see this. She may consider that I am doing a servant's work).

"I am invited everywhere and lovely people call, but that is because I am the niece of a wealthy woman. And yet people's love for Aunt Susan seems so genuine—not as though they were toadying to her for her money. And Grandmamma, 'Mr. Tom,' as I call him,—Tom Harper—is the

finest man I ever met.   He is a man—not a
man like Harvey Bigelow, mind you,—and
people respect him and look up to him.   He
comes here every other night.   He has a
buckboard and on Sundays he takes me for
long drives.   Doesn't he love Aunt Susan
though?   He told me that there never lived
such a good and unselfish woman, and then
he told me of all that she had done.

"His brother and he were left orphans
without a penny.   His father was a clergy-
man and his mother and Aunt Susan had
been friends for years;   in fact, he says,
'My mother had been one of Aunt Susan's
pupils.'   I must have shown surprise for
he answered when I said 'What?'—'Yes,
before her father died she taught in the
High School.'   Did you know it, Grandmamma?   Well, she did.   She's awfully in-
telligent and now I know the cause of it.
Why, she's like a walking dictionary.

"Mr. Tom said that his father and mother
died inside of a month, and he and his little
brother Fred were left alone.   Then brave
Aunt Susan, who had loved his parents,
came forward and legally adopted them.

Think, Grandmamma,—but for her they might have had to go to the Orphan Asylum and wear blue gingham uniforms.

"Then Aunt Susan sent them each to college.   Poor Fred contracted typhoid fever and died during his third year.   Mr. Tom and Aunt Susan say he was lovely— so gentle and sweet.   It is sad to die so young, isn't it?   But Mr. Tom graduated from college and studied law with Ex-Judge Green, and if you will believe it, all of the Judge's practice came to him at his death—Judge Green's death I mean—and he told me that he could never repay dear Aunt Susan for her goodness to him and to his brother.   It was more than that of a mother, for they were not of her blood.

"I'll close now, for Mr. Tom has come to take me for a long drive.   I hope the girls get in to see you often.   What do they think of Mamma's giving me permission to join Cousin Kate's Camp Fire Girls?   Isn't it great?

With love and lots of kisses to all,
        Your affectionate grandchild,
                    Ethel."

CHAPTER XIII

A LITTLE DRIVE

That afternoon when Tom took Ethel for a drive he asked: "Do you see that large house on the hill?"

"Yes," replied the girl. "It used to belong to Aunt Susan, didn't it?"

"It did," replied the man, "and she presented it to the town of Akron for an asylum for partially insane people—men and women who have hallucinations only—so that by gentle and humane treatment they may be helped if not permanently cured, for she believes that many who might gain their reason are made hopelessly insane by ill usage. She not only gave the house and land but she added to it a couple of wings, and she has created of it a most charming Sanitarium. I'll take you there tomorrow. You see, Aunt Susan gave it out that if the prominent business men of Akron could raise fifty thousand

dollars she would give fifty more, making
the sum total of one hundred thousand
dollars as a fund for the future support of
the Asylum, and by George!" said the
young man, "they raised it. So you see
so far as money is concerned they are inde-
pendent. The capital is invested in bonds
and stock, and the Asylum is run with the
dividends, and is well run, too. Aunt
Susan is the head—the President—and at
any moment she may surprise them and
walk in. The patients are treated with
courtesy and a great many are discharged
cured; in fact, nearly all. It accomodates
only fifty patients—twenty-five of each sex.
There's a continuous waiting list and it's
seldom that one isn't greatly benefited after
having gone there."

No wonder Aunt Susan was beloved by
the inhabitants, for Tom told Ethel that
she was invariably the first to help anyone
in distress.

"So she wasn't a miser, after all,"
thought the girl— "She gives away everything in charity and she saves her money
to do so."

Ethel couldn't fail to observe that Aunt
Susan was growing fond of her and her con-
science smote her. She felt that she was
a hypocrite. Even as she pondered she
held in her hand a letter received from her
mother which advised her to be tactful
and make herself agreeable and invaluable
to the old lady,—alter her gowns and make
and trim her hats, etc. "You're clever,
and from helping me sew you have become
proficient and have acquired considerable
knowledge of dressmaking. If she's mi-
serly and won't buy new, my child, you can
flatter her by remodeling her old gowns,
etc. Then she'll grow to depend on you.
She'll consider you a good manager and
feel that her money will not be wasted by
you. Then, when you marry we'll go
abroad to associate with peers and duch-
esses and members of the nobility. You'll
feel that your period of imprisonment with
Aunt Susan has brought forth fruit."

With a flushed face Ethel read and re-
read her mother's letter. She blushed with
shame. Already she had remodeled some
of Aunt Susan's gowns. She was glad that she

had done so before the letter came. From an old silk tissue skirt she had fashioned her a lovely neckpiece with long ends. She had also made her a dainty hat of fine straw and lace. She had persuaded her to allow her to dress her hair which grew quite thick on her head. First, as her hair had originally been black, she washed and *blued* it, making it like silver. Then, parting it in front, she waved it either side and coiled it loosely in the back, and really Aunt Susan looked like another woman,—most lovely and aristocratic. Tom was delighted with the metamorphosis and insisted upon Ethel's taking twenty dollars from him to buy her aunt a new stylish wrap.

"Oh, I'm so glad it all happened before I received this," she said to herself, tearing up the letter. "At least I'm not so contemptible as I might have been had I done as Mamma suggested, for gain only."

CHAPTER XIV

SOME CONFIDENCES

Aunt Susan now looked up-to-date, younger and happier, and she was most grateful for everything that Ethel had done for her. They all went to theaters, moving picture shows, and twice a week Tom would hire a motor and they'd take long drives far into the country.

Ethel now knew why Aunt Susan loved the man so dearly. She praised him constantly and the girl thought: "Well, if as Dorothy Kip expresses it he's doing these kind acts to 'build character' with Aunt Susan, at least he's an excellent actor."

They visited the Insane Asylum. It was like a lovely summer hotel and the nurses were most solicitous and polite to the patients. Ethel could understand how they might be cured,—how their poor tired and sick brains were rested and strengthened by humane treatment. It was a wonderful

revelation to the young girl—this charity
of Aunt Susan's. What a good, worthy
woman, and after her death what a reward
awaited her if we are to be rewarded ac-
cording to our good deeds.

Ethel was changing. She had lost a good
deal of her worldly pride. Cousin Kate
was expected the following week and she
was looking forward to trying on her Camp
Fire costume, and to the happy days that
were to come.

One morning Aunt Susan sat by the
window sewing. She looked actually lovely,
or at least Ethel thought so, and longed for
Grandmamma to see the change that she had
wrought. As she gazed upon the old lady
she said to herself: "Perhaps, it is because I'm growing so fond of her."

Aunt Susan had on a white silk sacque that
Ethel had made, trimmed with rare old lace
ruffles at the wrist and collar, while her
hair was very white and pretty. There was
a gentle breeze blowing in at the window,
and little curly locks fell upon her forehead.

Ethel was knitting a sweater. She had
learned the stitch in the town where she had

bought her wool, and she was making one
for her mother. In after years she never
knitted that she didn't think of the conversation that took place between Aunt
Susan and herself. The ground was covered
with white petals of apple and cherry blos-
soms and it was as though the snow had
fallen in May. She remembered everything
connected with that conversation, and later
in life she could close her eyes and hear
the robins calling and see the butterflies
flitting among the bushes, for that morning
was the turning point in her life.

"Aunt Susan," began the girl, knitting
very rapidly, "Mr. Tom tells me that his
mother was your pupil. Did you teach
very long?"

"Yes, Ethel," she replied, "I taught for
years. Father, although a rich man, expected his girls to do something, and there
he was wise. He always said that a girl
should have some occupation the same as a
boy; then, when ship-wrecks came, they'd
know how to swim. In other words, when
one's money was taken away there would be
something to fall back upon. Your grandmother took music lessons and taught for

a while, but she was pretty and during her first visit to New York, Archie Hollister fell desperately in love and married her. Tom's mother was a fine character and my favorite pupil. In so many ways Tom resembles her. She was clever and bright, and so is Tom. Why, Ethel, he has more than paid me for what I have done for him and Freddie. Today he's not twenty-five and he's one of our cleverest lawyers. I shouldn't be surprised if some day Ohio would send him to Congress. You know some of our cleverest men come from this state,—presidents and statesmen''—and Aunt Susan's cheeks grew pink with excitement.

"And dear little Fred," she continued— "he was more like a baby. He sort of clung to me; but, Ethel, they were like my own children, and you've no idea how happy they made me."

"Aunt Susan," said Ethel, with her cheeks aflame, "don't think me impertinent but you seem different from an——"

"An old maid," laughed Aunt Susan, that's what you dared not say."

Ethel nodded and continued: "From the different photographs I have seen of you, you must have been lovely. Why have you never married?"

Aunt Susan blushed and said in a low voice: "Ethel, I have been married."

The girl started.

"Haven't you noticed that people call me *Mrs.* Carpenter?"

"Yes," replied the girl, drawing nearer with wonder in her eyes, "but I know several maiden ladies who are called 'Mrs.' Mamma has a second cousin—she's dead now, I mean—but I remember her. She speculated in Wall Street and had an office, and she insisted upon being called Mrs."

"Yes, I've heard of women like her," replied Aunt Susan, "but I married a man by the same name, although no relation. Has your grandmother never spoken of him?"

"Never," replied the girl.

"Well, Alice has always hidden the family skeleton, but I will tell you all about it.

"When I was about thirty-six years of age I married Robert Carpenter. I was alone

and wealthy. I loved him and tried to
make his life happy, but he drank. He had
inherited that habit from his father, and
drinking led to gambling. He grew worse
and worse. One night under the influence
of drink he came home and seemed determined to pick a quarrel. Seeing that
he was irresponsible I made no reply to his
very insulting remarks. That angered him
beyond endurance. He struck and threw
me across the room. Then he left the
house.

"Over on the hill by the Asylum is the
grave of my little son who was born and
died that night."

Ethel started.

"Yes, my dear, I have been a wife and
mother. Of course, I knew nothing until
the next day. I recovered consciousness
but Robert had gone. He had taken all of
my money that he could find in the house
and he had not gone alone. His companion was a disreputable woman from the
town."

Aunt Susan paused and looked over
toward the little grave on the hillside.

"It seemed," she continued, "as though God, who knew my sorrow at losing my little one, sent me my two dear boys—Tom and Fred. They came into my life when I most needed them and were my greatest comfort, for I was a lonely woman, my dear. One day I received a letter written in a strange hand saying that my husband was ill and not likely to live—that he wished for me, to ask my forgiveness, and he begged me for God's sake to go to him. I went. He was in Detroit in a squalid boarding house. I was shocked at the change. I had not realized that a man could so lose his good looks as he had done. I took him to a clean place kept by a woman who had been highly recommended. Upon my arrival he wept bitterly and begged my pardon. Then I was glad that I had never divorced him as my friends had advised, for the poor man had been deserted by his companion when the money had gone. He had kept on sinking lower and lower, ashamed to appeal to me until when what he thought to be his last illness came upon him he sent for me to ask my forgiveness."

"Did you give it?" asked the girl.

"Yes, Ethel, I did, and I gave it freely, because for the year past he had been stone blind. I was so glad that I could cheer him up and make the few remaining days of his life liveable."

"Did you ask him of his companion?" asked Ethel.

"No, he never spoke of her, nor did I. Had he wished to have told me he would have done so. Robert had many loveable traits—yes, many noble traits—but it was drink that ruined him. He was not mercenary. I had money, but until he began to drink he was too proud to take it from me. He was truly fond of me and would have married me had I been poor, but of course after he had started the downward course he lost his pride.

"Well, I joined him in Detroit and stayed until after he died. His sight never returned, but I read to him and cheered him up, and I had the satisfaction of knowing that I made the last part of his life happier. That's all, my dear. It is almost too sad to tell to a young girl."

Ethel sat and gazed upon her,—the
woman who had shown such mercy to a
brute,—a wife deserted by her husband,—a
mother never able to feel the hand of her
little child upon her cheek,—a woman
whose life had been spent in helping others,
with no thought of self. The tears came
into the girl's eyes. She seemed to behold
a bright halo about Aunt Susan's head,
and it filled her with awe. Suddenly she
saw herself as she really was,—the daughter
of a selfish, mercenary mother, whose sole
ambition was for her future position in life.
And this was her mission—to visit this
noble woman with a view to ingratiating
herself and becoming her heiress,—to make
her think she loved her,—to make herself
indispensable to her. Yes, those were her
mother's words. She had destroyed the
letter lest it should be seen, but she knew
it by heart. The young girl saw it all.
Her lips quivered and she felt so utterly
unworthy that she fell on her knees and
buried her face in Aunt Susan's lap, sobbing
bitterly.

CHAPTER XV

A NEW ETHEL

"Oh! Aunt Susan, you don't understand and I am afraid to tell you, but I am such a wicked girl—such a hypocrite, and so unworthy of your relationship and love. I am a cheater and a waster. My life is all lies and sham. It always has been lies and sham. I wish to tell you everything so that you may see me as I am.

"I came here to get into your good graces—to win your love that thereby I might gain your fortune and marry into one of our old families—a man of great social prominence—and I've been trying to make you like me and make myself necessary to you. I've tried to give you the impression that I was clever so that in case you wished to make me your heiress you would not hesitate for fear that I might be extravagant and a spendthrift. I can't tell you how bad I am. I've been ashamed of being seen with you on account of the queer way you dressed. I'm not fit to put my head in your lap—no, I'm not fit to stay under your roof any longer," and Ethel's sobs were pitiful to hear. She became hysterical. Then Aunt Susan took her in her arms.

"Child," she began, "don't cry. You have told me nothing new. I understood from the first why you came home with me. You have many noble traits of character. Your grandmother and I thought that under different influences you might become a splendid woman. It was she who suggested my inviting you. You are a good girl, Ethel, and above all you have a kind and tender heart. You are a Carpenter in spite of your mother, and anyone bearing my father's name can not go far from right. You have shown that this morning. Now, my dear, in this world environments have much to do with one's character, and you have never had a chance, my poor little girl," and Aunt Susan kissed and soothed her as a mother might have done. "Now forget it all, my dear child, just as I shall forget. Let us begin anew from this morning."

"But, Aunt Susan," sobbed the girl, "I feel so unworthy, and you are so sweet to forgive me. I should think you'd hate me and want me to leave your house. But, believe me, I do love you—I love you as dearly as I love Grandmamma and Papa. Excepting in books I never knew that any one woman could be so good and self-sacrificing as you are. Oh, will you believe that I don't want your money, and that I only care for your respect and forgiveness, and your love, if you can give it?"

"Yes, my dear, I believe every word that you say. I believe in you from now on," and Ethel threw her arms around Aunt Susan's neck and wept for joy.

CHAPTER XVI

AUNT SUSAN'S TRIALS

"And now sit down, my dear, and I will tell you something. First you can never be my heiress, for I have no money to give away or leave to anyone. Tom supports me entirely. You look surprised and I don't wonder. I never told your grandmother. She is old and, owning the house in New York as she does, would probably insist upon my living with her; and until a year ago I had hopes of recovering some of my property that I had been cheated out of, but I have given it up. I love pretty gowns and pretty things as well as anyone, but I am saving the money that Tom insists upon giving me to spend on myself for him. I wish to leave him something at my death. Now I will tell you about it and how I lost my fortune.

"At the time I adopted the boys I was a very wealthy woman. Previous to that year I had given away a great deal for charity, but I had a hobby and that hobby was to establish a humane Insane Asylum. I had seen so much cruelty practiced in different institutions where I happened to know some of the inmates, and I had heard of such shocking treatment received by patients, that I resolved to establish a reform. I gave my handsome home for the Asylum. I spent large sums in fitting it up, so that it might seem like a beautiful resort to the poor souls, and as Tom told you, I succeeded in what I undertook. The boys went through school and college,— or Tom did, and poor Fred would have graduated had he lived a year longer. It was sad that he had to die, and so young, too." Aunt Susan wept as she told of his death.

"Perhaps, you remember, Ethel, of reading or of hearing your father speak of the failure of the Great Western Cereal Company four years ago. No? I was under the impression that your father owned a few shares of stock. Well, all I possessed in the world was invested in that Company.

It produced the greatest excitement known
in years; in fact, throughout the entire West
there were panics. Everyone who had a
little money saved up bought stock. The
dividends were enormous, but they were
bogus; that is, they were paid to each one
from his or her own money. It was one of
those unprincipled concerns. They had
been after me for a long while. They knew
that I was honest, wealthy, and respected,
and that my name would attract. At first,
I put in only a few thousand; then, as it
prospered, I put in more, and finally I put
in all that I possessed, for I wished to make
another fortune that I might build more
'Homes' and do greater good to suffering
humanity. The week before its failure
what do you think? Three of the princi-
pals sailed for Europe. Two were caught,
tried and are now serving a long term in
prison. Two others committed suicide.
Being one of its directors, when the bubble
burst I gave up everything I possessed to
help pay some of its poorer creditors, but
it only went a little way; and I, too, was
a victim with the rest. Had I confided my

business to Tom he would have advised me
not to invest in it, for Tom has a wonderful
way of advising people for the best, but I
kept it a secret so that when he should come
of age I could surprise him, for then I intended to give him full charge of all my
affairs. So you see, Ethel, I may have
appeared close and penurious, but now you
understand why. Tom, although getting
on finely, works very hard for every penny,
and at times he is almost too generous."

"Oh, Aunt Susan," said the girl drying
her eyes, "I feel happy now that you know
all and don't despise me. I'm glad that
you're poor and that I shan't get any of
your money. I only wish that I might go
to college. Yes, I'd work my way through
to get a good education so that I could be
able to earn my living and not take everything from poor Papa, who works so hard,"
and Ethel kissed the old lady many times.

CHAPTER XVII

COUSIN KATE ARRIVES

Ethel was too loyal to read her mother's letters to Aunt Susan who always smiled when she received one, but Mrs. Hollister wrote often asking her how she was progressing.

"Aunt Susan writes Grandmother that she has grown to love you very dearly, Ethel, and I see that you have followed my advice like my own daughter. It is now the sixth of June; probably, you will go with Cousin Kate to camp soon. I wish it was all over. I don't like the idea at all. It will throw you in with a common set of girls, I'm sure. We have saved quite a little this summer by staying home. The girls come in when they are in town and Grandmother enjoys their visits. Mrs. Bigelow and I met on the Avenue. She inquired all about you and I told her that upon Aunt Susan's death you would proba-

bly be a very wealthy girl. She admires
you immensely and she told me in confidence
that Harvey says when you are a few years
older and 'come out' you will take Society
by storm."

Everyone in the younger set of Akron
liked Ethel. She acted in private theatri-
cals; she sang and played, attended teas,
and was sought after for bridge. She gave
card parties, and the young people raved
over the quaintness of the old-fashioned
house. She took long walks with Tom.
She inveigled him into high collars and dis-
carding shoestring ties or wearing cravats
in a bow with loose ends. She even per-
susaded him to give up slouch hats and
dress more up-to-date. He and Aunt Susan
dubbed her the "Rejuvenator and Re-
former," and she was contented and happy.

Cousin Kate arrived and Ethel was overjoyed upon seeing her, she looked so fine
and strong. Her father came with her just
to see 'Archie's girl,' and Ethel loved him
instantly. He was so like her father that
the tears came into her pretty eyes when
at the depot she kissed him goodbye.

CHAPTER XVIII

SELECTING THE COSTUME

"You like Father, don't you?" asked Kate of Ethel, as they briskly walked toward the shopping district.

"Like him!" replied the girl, "why, Kate, I just love him. He reminds me of Grandmamma and Papa, but he's more like Grandmamma."

"He *is* like her," replied her cousin, "and I tell you, Ethel, he's just a dear. But, by the way, wasn't Aunt Susan clever to get your mother to consent to your becoming a Camp Fire Girl? I was so surprised. You see I had already spoken to Grandmother and you about it. Then I thought I'd tell Aunt Bella and get her interested in it, and ask her to let you join *my* Camp Fire, for Uncle Archie promised me that you should come out to Ohio and make me a visit. I had it in my mind that were you to come this summer it would be

lovely for you to go with us to Camp, but
do you know, Aunt Bella didn't like it a
little bit; in fact, she became very angry,
nor could I convince her of the virtue of the
Camp Fires nor even the Scouts. She
made me promise not to mention the subject again, and on no account in your presence. As I was her guest, I promised.
What knowledge you had you received
before. In this case the 'end has justified
the means,' and it was consummated by
Aunt Susan, so it's all right. But here we
are. This is the store where they take
orders for Camp Fire costumes. It will
take four days to make what you need. We'll
have to hurry them as we leave in five."

"Oh, Kate," began Ethel in a worried
voice, "do you think that I should let Aunt
Susan pay for them. She was awfully generous to offer, but when I accepted I
thought that she was wealthy, you know,
and now it's different. I really feel as
though I should not accept."

"Do you wish my advice?" answered
Kate. "You accept them. Why, you
might offend her by refusing. It's her

pleasure to start you in this good work. She obtained your mother's consent and she wishes to present you with an outfit. Oh, no, it would not do to even demur. Besides, they are very inexpensive. If you wish, the ceremonial gown of khaki color you may buy yourself. It can be purchased by the yard and it's of galatea which is cheap. You are clever with your needle and you can embroider it with beads and shells. You can also make the leather trimming in no time, and there's your costume complete. But let her pay for the other. So come in and be measured."

The girls selected a blue cloth skirt with pockets. The skirt buttoned all the way up and down the front and back. They selected two blouses—serge and galatea—each matching the skirt. The waists were cut open in the neck. They also ordered a pair of blue serge bloomers to be used in camping or hiking. These with a hat completed the purchase.

The hat was of blue cloth with a silver grey "W" on a dark blue background. The "W" meant "Wohelo" and could be used as a cockade. The saleswoman explained to Ethel that an emblem of two brown crossed logs was to be worn on the chest of the blouses. Honors gained in water sports might be embroidered as decorations around the collar. The same crossed logs woven into a blue background were used as sleeve emblems. Ethel saw the sample suit and was charmed. The decorations were unique and stylish.

"Please send them direct to Columbus," said Kate, as she paid the bill, and turning she said to Ethel: "You will be there, and it will save time. They generally fit perfectly; if not, as you know something of sewing, we can alter them to fit."

"I guess I do know something of sewing," replied Ethel. "I can do beautiful work and I can ride horseback, and I'm at home on a 'bike'."

Cousin Kate laughed.

"Well, I'm glad of that, for at first when you start in you'll be a Wood-Gatherer. Three months is the regular time, but you will be living in camp and will probably be able to fulfil all requirements in a month.

Your knowing these things will help you too."

"Tell me something about it, Kate," said Ethel on their way home. "After you have been a "Wood Gatherer' you become a 'Fire Maker?'" she asked.

"Yes. When you first enter, the Guardian of your Camp Fire gives you a silver ring on which is engraved a bundle of seven fagots, representing the seven points of the law. You give her the size, your address, etc., and she gets it at Headquarters for you, announcing your desire to become one. You must promise not to sell nor give it away. It may belong only to a Camp Fire Girl. Upon your right arm, as you already know, are the crossed logs, etc. When you become a Fire Maker you may add the orange color to your Wood Gatherer's emblem. This color represents flame, and when you advance to the position of Torch Bearer you may add a touch of white which represents smoke from the flame. Then, while you are in that class, you may wear the Fire Maker's bracelet. 'Fire' is the symbol of our organization. For decorative purposes it may be represented by the rising sun.

"Now the symbol of membership is the tall pine tree. That stands for simplicity and strength. Of course, you know the watchword—'Work, Health, and Love.' The first two letters of each form the one word 'Wohelo.' After joining you'll learn everything.

"Honors are symbolized by different colored beads—'Health craft,' bright red beads; 'Home craft,' orange; 'Nature love,' sky blue; 'Camp craft,' wood brown; 'Hand craft,' green; 'Business,' black and gold; and 'Patriotism,' red, white and blue. These, and the seven laws, are represented by the seven fagots on the ring. The beads are strung on leather and may become part of the ceremonial dress.

"Now the name of my Camp Fire is 'Ohio.' It is an Indian name and means 'beautiful.' You know Ohio is called the 'Buckeye State,' Buckeye meaning 'Ohio Horse-Chestnuts.' Unlike your horse-chestnut, our tree is small and its flower is red. So our 'totem' or symbol is 'Buckeye,' or the 'Horse-Chestnut.'

"The girls are to meet at our house the night before we start. Then you can learn the sign, how to keep count, and the different poems you are to say; and the 'Wohelo' ceremony, toasts, songs, etc. This is all that I shall tell you now. Our camp is near the Muskingum river. We have no very high elevations in Ohio. The highest is only about fifteen hundred feet. Where we go is a pleasant stretch of woods. There we camp out for a month or so. A clearing has been made; we can put up tents and be very comfortable. It is not far from a small town and the girls can walk in when they choose. Other 'Camp Fires' will be there as well, so there will be no lack of society. But, my dear girl, if I were you I'd join one in New York and keep steadily at it. It's the only way to become proficient and gain honors and advancement, and that's your aim, isn't it?"

"It is, Kate," replied the girl, "I shall surely join this fall. An aunt of one of the girls in our set is a Guardian of eight girls or more, and she's simply lovely. I shall certainly keep it up—never you fear."

CHAPTER XIX

ETHEL MEETS HER UNCLE AND AUNT

Aunt Susan was most interested in the description of the costume, its symbols, etc. Ethel thanked her gratefully for her gift, impulsively kissing her many times. The elderly woman had grown very fond of the girl and dreaded parting with her, but she knew that the new work she was about to take up would be of the greatest benefit to her, not only then but in the future, for Ethel had softened wonderfully. She had lost all of her false pride and worldliness. It was as though a new girl had arisen from the ashes of the old one, and now she stood revealed as Nature had intended her—without sham,—and knowing that it was she who had helped to bring it about, Aunt Susan was happy. She was proud of the two girls—her grandnieces,— Ethel with the delicate beauty of a bud, while Kate appeared and reminded her of

a full blown rose. She was tall and finely
formed, with hair that envious people often
termed red, but it really had escaped being
red and was auburn. The girl wore it in
coils around her shapely head. Her eyes
were of the softest brown, while Ethel's
were of a deep blue. Each girl had regular
features and fine teeth. They resembled
each other to that extent that they were
often taken for sisters, and Tom was proud
of them as well and was delighted to take
them out.

"Why," he'd say, "when I'm out with
you two girls everyone makes such a fuss
over me that I really feel as though I was
'somebody,' and I know it's all on your
account. The fellows come up and say
'Harper, old man, I haven't seen you for an
age,' or, 'Harper, I heard of you through so
and so last week. I wish to congratulate
you on that case, etc.' But I know what it
means,—they want an introduction to you
girls—and I strut around like a peacock."

But the day for their departure arrived
only too soon.

"I'll write every other day to you,

Auntie," called Ethel from the car window.

"How about writing to me?" shouted Tom.

"Once a week to you, Tom," laughed Ethel.

Uncle John Hollister met them at the depot and Ethel at once fell in love with Kate's mother, who seemed more like the girl's sister. They vied with one another to give Ethel a good time and she enjoyed every moment. She met the Camp Fire girls, some of whom were charming. Two of the girls—Mattie Hastings and Honora Casey—she did not care for. To her they seemed unlike the others and she found herself saying mentally, "They are extremely common; I wonder where Kate picked them up," immediately after which she would become ashamed.

"I'm going back into my old ways," she thought. "These girls are to be my sisters and companions. I *must* like them."

Honora had a large red face, partially freckled. Her voice was loud and coarse. She seemed to be one of the "nouveau riche," as Ethel's mother was wont to say of people grown suddenly wealthy and prosperous. Yet Ethel was not alone in her dislike of the girl. No one seemed to care for her, although each member treated her politely.

Mattie Hastings had small eyes that never seemed to look you quite fully in the face. She had also an obsequious manner. At times it was fairly repellant.

"I wouldn't trust her," Ethel said to Kate one evening.

"She's not popular, I admit, and her manner is against her, but, Ethel, I have never found a fault in her; that is, one I could criticise. She is very quick to learn and seems ambitious. She came to me and asked if she might join. They are poor but her people are respectable. Now Honora Casey's parents are the wealthiest people here. They came into their wealth suddenly. The father is a builder and contractor. The mother is hurting the girl by her method of trying to get into society. She fairly pushes everything before her. Mr. Casey, or Pat Casey, as he is called, is a good-hearted Irishman. He is sensible

and knows that it is his money that buys
everything, even social standing, for although much respected he is a man of no
education, nor has his wife any more than
he, but she tries to bluff it through, therefore she is not popular. Nora has been
educated, or half educated, at a Convent.
She never graduated, but she's so good-
hearted one can overlook her mother's
faults. You see, Ethel, it takes all sorts of
people to make a world. We must try to
excuse their failings and see only the best in
them. Of course, you know we are an old
family of good standing and can go where
we choose. Perhaps it was on that account
that Mrs. Casey made Nora join my Camp
Fire Girls, but she seemed most anxious
that she should. It doesn't matter much.
She'll make a fine woman if she sticks to
her work. You see, our organization is
most democratic. One has only to express
a wish and she may become a member."

"The other girls are lovely," said Ethel.
"I think Patty Sands is charming."

"Isn't she?" responded Kate. "Her
father is an ex-Congressman. He is Judge

of the Supreme Court. He didn't care
for politics—refused the second term.''

''Yes, I suppose it is poor taste for me
to even criticise the girls, but every once
in a while the old bad habit comes back
and I forget my good resolutions. At
heart they are probably far better girls than
I, but I do wish that Mattie Hasting's eyes
were not so close together.''

CHAPTER XX

That evening the girls met in Kate Hollister's library. Although it was June and there was a log fire in the fireplace it was not warm. The girls carried a small flag upon which the word "Ohio" was embroidered, and underneath appeared a horse-chestnut. Each girl had made her own flag and they were well done.

That afternoon Kate had taken her cousin to the Camp Fire counsel, where, upon her signifying the desire to become a member, the silver ring had been presented to her.

After order had been established and the roll called, Kate, who made a dignified Guardian, began to addresss the girls, formally introducing her cousin, the new member. Then Ethel repeated the following:

"It is my desire to become a Camp Fire

Girl and to obey the Law of the Camp Fire, which is

Seek beauty,
Pursue knowledge,
Give service,
Be trustworthy,
Hold on to health,
Glorify work,
Be happy.

"This Law of the Camp Fire I will strive to follow."

Then she took her seat while Kate arose and explained the Law, phrase by phrase, after which Ethel stood before her and repeated the Wood Gatherer's Desire, whereupon she taught Ethel the 'sign' which was made by flattening the fingers of the right hand against those of her left, which indicates crossed logs. From the first position, Ethel raised her right hand and followed the curves of an imaginary flame. Kate explained that this sign was used by the early American Indians. It may be made easier by placing the fingers of the right hand across those of the left with the forefinger slightly raised. Ethel

learned how to use the sign and practiced
it, after which Kate presented or awarded
honors to the various girls who had worked
for them.   They were only the different
colored beads, but each girl's eyes beamed
with happiness as she received them.

Then they showed Ethel the "Count"
book, in which were kept records of their
work and play.   The leaves were of brown
paper and laced together with a leather
thong or cord.   The cover was of leather
also.   Symbolic charts for recording the
requirements of the Fire Maker and Torch
Bearer, as well as for nearly two hundred
Elective Honors, were parts of the book.
The book contained ninety-six pages.   It
was arranged for a group of twelve girls.
Should the group grow larger, more leaves
could be added.   Three leaves for each girl
were in the first part of the book.   These
were for recording the honors and requirements, making thirty-six pages.   The bal-
ance of the pages were for the records of
events, pictures, and pen and ink sketches,
etc.

The totem of the Camp Fire is as painted

on the brown leather cover. It should always tell some legend or story—some natural industry or beauty which is true to the locality in which the Camp Fire is located. The "Ohio" Camp Fire totem was a large horse-chestnut under the word "Buckeye." The first leaf was left blank; the second was the title leaf upon the top of which appeared the name of the Camp Fire, and at the bottom the date of the first council fire; following the title leaf each girl fills out her group of three leaves. On the first she will write her name, date of birth, parents' names, birthplace, and present address. She also puts down the date as she attains each rank, using for the month the Indian name. On the next leaf were symbols of all Elective Honors, and these were painted in colors corresponding to the beads received. The third leaf for each girl was for her individual symbol,—the chosen name with its meaning,—for each girl naturally wishes to own some name by which she may be known. She may hold some desire which to her may mean the way in which she may give of her-

self the best. Perhaps some poem has
lines which she feels are a response to her
desire. Not only could these girls write
what happened and insert photographs
of their excursions, but they were at liberty
to make pen pictures along the margin of the
leaves of the book—all Indian signs from a
moon to a snake, telling of a trip to Rat
snake Pond, etc. They were to use the
rythm of Hiawatha, which after a little
practice becomes the natural language for
some girls and it adds much to the interest of the Count; for instance,

"Supper over, now they hasten
To their wigwams, all excitement,
And from hence soon reappearing
Now true Indian maidens seem they,"
etc.

"Now that we have initiated our new
member," said Kate, "and have explained
to her about the Count book, etc., we shall
postpone the rest of the ceremonies until
we reach Camp, as I know that each one
of you will need your rest. So we'll meet
at the train for the boat landing at eleven
tomorrow. I hope it will be a fair day.

Take plenty of wraps along for it is cold tonight and it bids fair to be so tomorrow."

Then saying good-night to each as they left the room, Kate and Ethel found themselves alone in front of the dying fire.

CHAPTER XXI

THE TRIP UP THE RIVER

It turned out to be a lovely day. Ethel was most excited. The tents, cooking utensils, pillows, cots, etc., had been sent two days before by freight. The trunks alone remained to be taken to the boat, and they were only steamer trunks.

Uncle John went along to see them safely on board the train that connected with the small boat that plied daily up the Muskingum river.

"If you get homesick, little one," he said to Ethel, "you come right back to us. Don't you stay if you don't like it."

"Oh, Uncle John, how could I get homesick with Kate?" she replied; "but I shall miss you awfully."

The whistle blew and away they went. It was a pretty sail and the girls were in a happy frame of mind. Nora Casey looked like one immense freckle. She was in high

spirits and now and then relapsed into a
jolly brogue caught from her parents, for
Nora was born in America.

"Faith and it's sailing that I enjoy,"
she said to Ethel, coming up the stairway
from the deck below. "I'm afther taking
some pictures of the river for our Count
book." Then catching herself she talked
perfectly correct without the slightest trace.

They watched the banks on either side,
dotted now and then by pretty houses and
thriving fields of buckwheat and clover.

Patty Sands sat by Ethel. They were
very congenial. The rest of the girls chat-
tered together. Mattie Hastings sat beside
Kate Hollister and regarded her with adoring
looks. Nora chatted excitedly; once in a
while Kate would check her exuberance of
spirits, as her voice could be heard by
people on the shore. Said Kate:

"Girls, there are several beautiful legends
connected with this river. I read a new
one the other day. At our first Camp Fire
I'll relate it. We can copy it in our book
under our totem. Suppose each of you
girls write an original legend and read it
aloud some rainy night."

"Good for Miss Hollister!" cried Honora. "We will."

So they promised.

Soon the journey came to an end. A four-seated buckboard stage had been engaged by Uncle John to meet the party and carry them up the steep hill into camp.

"Oh, isn't this jolly?" said Ethel enthusiastically. "What lovely woods!"

And indeed they looked like a picture with the June sunshine every now and then bursting through the trees. The road was narrow but it was a good road for walking. The old buckboard creaked and groaned with its load of eight girls, their Guardian, and the driver. Every once in a while the horses would stop and the driver dismount and with his handkerchief wipe off the white sweat that looked like soapsuds.

"He's a kind man," said Kate.

Then when his handkerchief was too wet to use he would pick up handfuls of grass to use for their comfort, after which he would get up on the seat and drive them again, but he must have stopped ten times before reaching the clearing where the Camp was to be.

"Oh, look!" cried Patty. "Miss Hollister, our four tents are up."

"Yes, that's Father's surprise," she rejoined. He sent up one of his men yesterday so that we need have no trouble." And turning to Ethel she said: "Usually we have to hire a man in the village to come up and do such work, but Father has anticipated us this time."

"Isn't he lovely?" said the girls in unison, jumping like children from the wagon and peeping into each tent. There were all the baskets ready to be unpacked, and following the buckboard came the trunks.

They quickly removed their hats, etc., and bade the driver goodbye, who by the way was now using handfuls of leaves to clean the animals; after which each one was assigned her task.

"Patty Sands, you may unpack and wipe the china. Mattie Hastings, you may put it in place. Ethel, you may watch this time, as you are a tenderfoot. Nora, you arrange the blankets, towels, and linen in order, will you?" And so Kate kept each girl working.

Mollie Long made the cots; Sallie Davis put the cooking utensils in place; Edith Overman and Edna Whitely began gathering sticks for the fire.

"Oh!" ejaculated Ethel, "that's my task, isn't it? I'm the Wood Gatherer," she said.

"The first day a tenderfoot is our guest," replied Mollie Long, laughing. "You wander away and think of the story you'll have to write and read aloud."

"In other words," broke in Nora, "go way back and sit down."

But Ethel watched the girls work. It was a revelation to her. They seemed more like boys.

"Why," explained Edna Whitely, "if necessary we could drive the stakes and put up our tent, couldn't we, Miss Hollister?"

"Yes, I hope you'd be able to," she said. "I think women do far harder work than that every day."

Kate had changed her gown for a pair of bloomers and was working hard running back and forth giving orders like a general.

By twilight every trunk was unpacked and in its place. Each girl had changed her gown and the Camp Fire was ready to light after tea. Then came preparations. In one tent there was an oil stove. Outside stood a barrel of oil. It was an extra tent to be used as a kitchen. Two upright stakes with one running across, upon which were many hooks, served to hold all of the kitchen utensils. They hung from it as naturally as though in a real kitchen. One of the packing boxes became a serving table and afterwards did duty for a sink. In the center of the kitchen was a long table made of planks laid upon a wooden horse at either end. When pleasant the girls preferred to eat outside, sitting Indian fashion, but when rainy the kitchen tent made an admirable shelter.

CHAPTER XXII

AN EVENING IN CAMP

The supper was prepared by the Fire
Makers,—Edith Overman, Patty Sands,
and Mattie Hastings. Patty baked a couple
of large pans of delicious biscuits. Mattie
made tea and eggs scrambled with cheese.
Edith Overman boiled some rice for dessert
so that each flake stood alone and was
creamy, upon which the girls put butter
and sugar or butter and maple syrup.
Later in the season they picked berries and
had them for tea.

The meal was well cooked and they enjoyed it. Ethel cleared the table. Sallie
Davis and Mollie Long washed the dishes,
while Nora and Edna Whitely tidied up the
tent, after which the fire was lighted with
the usual ceremony. Ethel as a Wood
Gatherer insisted upon bringing the twigs,
wood and kindling. The Fire Maker—
Edna Whitely—arranged them ready to

light.   Kate chanted a command to Mollie
Long and Nora Casey, who were Torch
Bearers.

In the meanwhile each one seated her-
self around the fire.   Mollie and Kate then
came forward, and by rubbing two sticks
together ignited the paper under the shav-
ings, and soon there burst up a beautiful
flame.   Then the girls arose and repeated:
   "Burn, fire, burn,
  Flicker, flicker, flame,
  Whose hand above this blaze is lifted
  Shall be with magic touch engifted
  To warm the hearts of lonely mortals
  Who stand without their open portals:
  The torch shall draw them to the fire,
  Higher, higher,
  By desire.
  Whoso shall stand by this hearthstone
  Flame fanned
  Shall never, never stand alone;
  Whose house is dark and bare and cold,
  Whose house is cold,
  This is his own.
  Flicker, flicker, flicker, flame,
  Burn, fire, burn."

After which Edna repeated the Fire Maker's song:

> "As fuel is brought to the fire,
> So I purpose to bring
> My strength,
> My ambition,
> My heart's desire
> My joy
> And my sorrow
> To the fire
> Of humankind;
> For I will tend,
> As my fathers have tended,
> And my fathers' fathers
> Since time began,
> The fire that is called
> The love of man for man,
> The love of man for God."

They gave toasts, told stories and sang songs. Edith Overman had a keen sense of humor and she told some anecdotes that were exceedingly droll. Ethel and Edna Whitely vied in asking conundrums. Kate Hollister then related her capital story, "The Legend of the Muskingum."

"Before I begin," she said, "for Ethel's

benefit I wish to tell you something of the
origin of the Camp Fire. This I read in a
New York magazine.

" 'If we go back as far as possible we
come to a primitive time when human life
centered about the Camp Fire. It was,
and is still, the center of family life, and
today it is around the fire that the family
and friends gather. The fire gives warmth
and cheer to the home. The day's work is
begun with fire. When the fire is out the
house is cheerless. Fire stands for Home—
for the Community Circle and New Patriotism. It was also in these primitive days
that the first grand division of labor was
made. The man,—the provider and de-
fender of the family—went out into the
wilderness to hunt, while the woman stayed
at home to keep the pot boiling, and in
spite of all of the changes in social life that
division has remained to a very large extent
until this day.

" 'Some years ago, when the Boy Scout
movement first started, it began with the
Camp Fire. No doubt one reason for its
popularity was the fact that it gave the boys

opportunity to play what was in the old
days the man's game—that of hunter,
trapper, and soldier.

" 'Boys may be Scouts, but you girls
are going to keep the place to which the
Scout must return. And now this movement, similar to the Boy Scouts, has been
started for girls. It started also with the
Camp Fire, and the organization thus
formed is the Camp Fire Girls.' "

Everyone clapped their hands.

"When I read the above," said Kate,
"I learned it by heart, knowing that all of
you would be interested to know the true
significance of the Camp Fire. And now
for the Legend."

CHAPTER XXIII

THE LEGEND OF THE MUSKINGUM RIVER

"Long years ago there lived a brave Indian chief called Wa-chi-ta; in fact, he and his tribe inhabited a portion of this state—perhaps in the vicinity of these very trees.

"He was a kind and humane man, and his wife, Ona-pas-see, was like him in that respect, therefore they were dearly beloved by their subjects. They had three fine sons but no daughter, so when a little girl came to them they were exceedingly happy and there was great rejoicing.

" 'As she is fair and beautiful to behold we will call her O-hi-o,' said the Chief. ("As we know, Ohio means 'beautiful,' " said Kate.)

"So little O-hi-o waxed strong and grew into a woman worthy of her name. She was idolized by Ona-pas-see and spoiled by Wa-chi-ta.

"After the manner of all maidens, when

she arrived at the marriageable age from
miles around came many braves to pay
their respects. They brought her rare and
costly gifts of silver, copper, and gold—of
beads and bears' claws, as well as the skins
of the fox, squirrel, and ermine.

"O-hi-o smiled sweetly and accepted her
gifts with pretty speeches of thanks, but
of the young men she would have none.
Her parents worried not a little, as they
wished to see her settled in life, living in her
own wigwam. Her brothers talked with
her upon her duty, but she only smiled,
showing her pretty teeth and arranged her
headband of beads, using for a glass the
clear stream near the wigwam.

"The squaws declared that she would
never marry—that soon would go her
youth and good looks; then the braves
would seek some maiden younger and
fairer. But O-hi-o only shook her head and
ran to her father to be kissed.

" 'She is proud,' they said, gazing after
her, 'No one is good enough for her. She
will meet with her punishment—watch.'

"Then behold! there came to the village

one day a young warrior—Mus-kin-gum
by name. He came from a tribe many
miles distant, bearing a message from its
Chief to Wa-chi-ta.

"O-hi-o sat near her father. She was
embroidering a wampum belt with different
colored beads and shells, skilfully fashioning
birds, butterflies, animals, etc. As she
glanced up shyly, lo! her eye caught the
eye of the young brave. The blood flew
into her cheeks and her heart started in to
beat as though it would burst. While de-
livering his speech to Wa-chi-ta young
Mus-kin-gum grew scarlet and embarrassed.

"That was the beginning. It was in
June. The birds sang their love songs and
the air was filled with mysterious romance
and sweetness. Permission had been
granted by Wa-chi-ta to Mus-kin-gum to
pay his addresses to his daughter O-hi-o,
and when he told her of his love he said:

" 'Why confess it? You have known
since the day in the wigwam when our eyes
met and my soul fell captive to your beauty
and sweetness.'

"Then, when upon the mountain sides

the trees hung out their yellow, gray and
scarlet banners, with great pomp and ceremony these two young people were wed,
and the festivities lasted for days. Everyone was happy because Wa-chi-ta was
happy, and all of the tribe loved Wa-chi-ta.

"As for O-hi-o and Mus-kin-gum, they
were content. They lived in a fine wigwam and adored each other. While her
husband was in the woods shooting game or
fishing, Ohio would sit in the doorway and
watch for his return, and as for him, his
eyes were constantly roving towards the
valley where he could see the smoke coming
from a certain wigwam; and when it came
in volumes as though from a freshly started
fire, his heart would rejoice, for then he knew
that O-hi-o was preparing the supper and it
was time to return.

"And so these two who loved each other
lived in one continual honeymoon until the
arrival of little Mus-kin-gum—a strong,
lusty, little fellow looking not unlike Wa-
chi-ta, which pleased his grandfather only
too well. It was his father's delight to
attend to his education, and his father was

not only beloved by his tribe but feared by his enemies. So he wished to teach his little son to be honest, kind and fearless. He wished him to be brave and able to lead his tribe into battle—to die for them if necessary. He taught the boy to aim well and shoot with a bow and arrow, and when he was about seven years old it was his delight to accompany big Mus-kin-gum on his shooting expeditions—to help him fish and hunt. Together they would tramp for miles, and O-hi-o would sit in her doorway and embroider, thanking the Great Spirit that she had two warriors to look after instead of one; and little Mus-kin-gum would clap his hands with joy when she'd say:

" 'What has the little warrior shot to-day?' And her husband would reply: 'He has helped me; he has carried my heavy bow and arrow; and he has also carried these,' displaying a large string of fish. 'Besides, he caught two of them.'

"Of course, they talked in Indian language, which is more beautiful than ours.

"Then on their trips Mus-kin-gum would

teach his little son how to distinguish one tree from another by examining its leaves; how to tell the name of a bird by listening to its call; how to read the signs of the Indians; how to read from their tracks the whereabouts of the enemy, the trail of the animals, and the secrets of the woods—the song of the birds, the whispering of the trees, and the murmuring of the brook; about the way of flowers, ferns, etc., and the names of the different nuts and fruits that flower first and then become ripe and fall to the ground.

"He taught him about the different animals and how to trap and shoot them, and lastly he taught him about the stars and the stories connected with them. Little Mus-kin-gum could point out the Dipper or Great Bear, the Little Bear, how the last star but one in the Dipper—the star at the bend of the handle—is called 'Mizar,' one of the horses; and just above tucked close in is a smaller star—'Alcor' or 'the rider.' The Indians called these two the 'Old Squaw and the Papoose on her back,' and the young men would say to the little fellow: 'Do you see the papoose on the old squaw's back?'

"Then at once he'd point to them, and the parents would be proud of him.

"His father also taught him that shaking a blanket in Indian language meant 'I want to talk with you.' Holding up a tree branch—'I wish to make peace.' Holding up a weapon—'I am prepared to fight,' and many others like our own signal of the Camp Fires," said Kate, "which is one of the oldest of Indian signs."

"Isn't this a lovely story?" broke in Patty. "I can't wait for its finish."

"And it's late; I'll have to talk more rapidly, I fear," replied Miss Hollister, "or postpone the rest until tomorrow night."

"Oh, don't," went up a shout of young voices,—"please finish. Why, we'd keep awake all night if you stopped now."

Kate laughed good-naturedly and signed to one of the Fire Makers to put on more wood. Quickly Ethel jumped up and brought an armful, for our Camp was very ceremonious. Then as the flame burst forth anew she proceeded:

"So you can see that little Mus-kin-gum
was a loveable child, endowed with more
than ordinary intelligence. His father also
told him of the Great Spirit, and the child
listened reverently. He was an unusual
child—bright for his age— and he learned
quickly. He was also affectionate, and
Mus-kin-gum became as weak as a woman
when the little fellow would put his arms
about his neck or clasp him by the hand.

"The mother had taught the child a
prayer to the Great Spirit. It was this:

" 'Great Spirit, listen Thou to us; guide
us this day; help us, lest we fall; make our
will Thy will—our ways Thy way.'

"Mus-kin-gum's great fear was that he
might lose him ere he grew up to manhood,
for next to O-hi-o he adored his boy.

"One morning big and little Mus-kin-gum
started for the woods. They were in high
spirits as they kissed O-hi-o goodbye.

" 'We will shoot for you a big deer,' said
the boy, 'and we will bring to you many
large fish.'

"O-hi-o smiled and wished them luck.
After watching until out of sight she left

her wigwam to spend the day with her parents. It was a warm June day and it reminded O-hi-o of her courting days. She lived it all over again, and her heart gave thanks to the Great Spirit for His kindness—for the wonderful love and happiness that had since been hers in the possession of her husband and child. And the birds sang as on the day that Mus-kin-gum first beheld her at the door of her father's wigwam. She could see his eyes holding her own; she could feel her heart bounding in her bosom, and the red flushed into her cheek even as it had done then.

"She spent a pleasant day talking of her two dear ones and her parents were never weary of listening. They made her repeat the little prayer said to the Great Spirit by the idolized grandson.

" 'I must leave now,' she said, 'and prepare their supper. They will be watching in the valley for the smoke from our wigwam,' and kissing her parents fondly she left.

"In the meanwhile it grew dark.

" 'Little one,' said Mus-kin-gum, 'we must hasten. I feel rain in the air. Look at the clouds and behold it in them ready to fall.'

"And the little fellow looked and laughed, thinking it fun to be caught in a shower. They were close to the edge of the woods ready to descend the path leading to the valley, when suddenly with terrific force the rain began to fall, followed by a mighty wind that rent the clouds and rushed through the woods. Thunder pealed loud and long; lightning flashed, blinding the eyes. Little Mus-kin-gum grew pale and trembled. Never before had he feared a storm.

" 'It is the voice of the Great Spirit,' he said solemnly, and began to repeat the prayer.

"Seeing his fright, his father drew the boy's head to his breast and held it there so that he might not see the lightning as it flashed with unusual violence.

"At last one flash came, and with it went the spirit of brave Mus-kin-gum. His arms loosened their hold on the screaming child. He reeled and fell backward—dead. The last bolt had killed him.

"Then followed peal after peal of thunder. The boy called to him in vain. He even tried to raise him in his arms. Seeing that it was useless he threw himself on his breast and moaned, every now and then lamenting in loud cries.

"The storm ceased. When, after the night fell, and Mus-kin-gum and the boy failed to appear, O-hi-o gathered together a band of young men from nearby and started out to search for them. O-hi-o kept calling, 'Mus-kin-gum, where art thou? My little one—art thou safe?'

"Then on the air floated a child's voice calling to its mother.

"Like a deer, O-hi-o flew to the spot. The child was rubbing his eyes. He had fallen asleep on his dead father's breast and was awakened by his mother's voice, but he never left his father's body.

"As O-hi-o drew near she beheld her poor brave handsome Mus-kin-gum lying with his face upturned to the moon, whose beams fell upon him. O-hi-o knelt down and kissed her husband but she uttered no cry—only a dull muffled moan escaped her, for she was the daughter of an Indian

Chieftain and it would not have done.
She had been taught to bear pain without
a murmur, but the look upon her face was
terrible. The young men would gladly
have died to have brought young Mus-kin-
gum to life for her sake.

"Then the eldest lifted the child, who
still sat by his dead father's side, and placed
him in his mother's arms, and as the little
fellow sobbed and kissed her lo! her eyes
filled with tears and she headed the pro-
cession that followed bearing the body of
their beloved Mus-kin-gum adown the steep
path that led to her wigwam.

"And Mus-kin-gum was buried with
great ceremony and honors becoming a
a man of his station. But O-hi-o took no
further interest in life. The child now
clung to his grandfather, who tried to take
his father's place. Every day O-hi-o would
lead him to the grave on the mountain side,
and together they would pray to the Great
Spirit.

" 'And I prayed in the woods,' said the
boy, 'when the thunder rolled and the
lightning came, but the Great Spirit turned
away his face and took my father.'

" 'He was called to live among the stars,'
O-hi-o would reply.

" 'And is he up there?' " the child would
ask. 'I will look for him,' after which
every night would little Mus-kin-gum stand
or lie on the ground gazing at the stars,
declaring at times that he could discern
his father looking down upon them.

"But alas! from the day of the storm the
boy could never again hear the voice of
thunder, nor see the flashes of lightning,
without going into convulsions. Upon the
first distant roar he would jump up and
down, scream loudly, and run to his mother,
burying his head on her breast, relapsing
into a state of semi-consciousness until the
storm should have passed. It was pitiful,
and poor O-hi-o's tears would fall on the
boy's head, for it was thus he had stood before his father while Mus-kin-gum met his
death.

"As time went on the attacks grew
worse. Vainly did old Wa-chi-ta summon
the best known medicine men and old
women, but each one shook his or her head
doubtfully. Vainly did the tribe assemble

in the Council wigwam to consult with one another and pray to the Great Spirit for Mus-kin-gum's son—for his recovery. Nothing seemed to avail. The child grew worse and worse, never caring to leave his mother's side.

"Then came a bad year for the Indians. There was a drought. The fruit fell from the trees while yet in flower. The grass turned brown and withered. The crops died. The water dried up and there was none for the cattle. The different tribes met and prayed with no result.

" 'We must die,' they said. 'Behold! the Lake even has gone, and something must be done.'

"And the wise men declared that the Great Spirit must be angry with them and that he demanded of them a sacrifice. The more they talked the more they believed that it was imperative. 'One life must be sacrificed,' they said,—'one life for many. That is the only way to save our people. No rain has fallen in nearly four months. The Great Spirit demands and must be obeyed.'

"Then into the midst of the wise men and chieftains came O-hi-o. She was very beautiful and the braves held their breath as they gazed upon her. By her hand she led the son of Mus-kin-gum.

" 'I have heard what you said—oh! wise men,' she began. 'I have no wish to live longer. I and my son are ready to be your sacrifice. My heart is in the grave upon the mountain side. My son is not strong; his health is poor. We give ourselves for the good of our people.'

"Many wept. The wise men regarded her as they might an angel sent by the Great Spirit. Her parents gazed upon her with pride and adoration.

" 'But,' she continued, 'I would choose the manner of my death. On the pinnacle of rocks overlooking this valley, where each day that he hunted in the woods my dear Mus-kin-gum would stand and wave to me, tomorrow night 'neath the light of the moon, with my son's hand in mine—together he and I will leap from that rock into the valley below,—the once lovely valley now so desolate. Do not refuse me,' she

cried, as many protested suggesting others
not so young. 'No, I will gladly make the
sacrifice for my dear father's people.'

"So they counselled together and accepted the offer made by their Chieftain's
daughter.

"O-hi-o and Mus-kin-gum spent their
last day with the old people, who, while
filled with pride, were heartbroken. They
clung to the mother and child, nor were
they ashamed to show their love and
weakness.

" 'I shall be with my father,' said little
Mus-kin-gum. 'You may look for my mother
and me in the stars, Grandpa. I have seen
father there. Be sure and watch; we shall
all be together,' and the child smiled as he
kissed his grandparents, whose hearts were
breaking.

" 'My two brave ones,' said old
Wa-chi-ta, 'if the rain comes to us it will
be you who have sent it.'

"The tribes assembled from miles around.
It was a hot, torrid night, although the moon
shone brightly. All was silent as O-hi-o
and little Mus-kin-gum came forth to the

sacrifice. She wore her ceremonial costume; her long, black hair was flowing and
held in by a beaded head-band. She
looked so beautiful as she marched up the
mountain that people wept, but she walked
proudly with her head erect, leading her
child by the hand, and the little fellow also
held his head upright and seemed without
fear. Soon the ledge was reached. Looking down into the valley below they took
their position.

" 'Farewell,' said O-hi-o, 'I do this for
the love I bear you, my people.'

"Then she kissed the boy many times
and, reconsidering, she lifted him in her
arms. The child put his face to hers and
clung tightly about her neck. She whispered in his ear. He raised his head and
called aloud: 'May the rain fall and may
you all be happy.'

"Then holding her child close to her
heart the brave woman stepped to the edge,
closed her eyes, and leaped into the valley
below,—the valley in which stood her wigwam."

Kate paused. The girls were hanging

breathlessly on her words. Sallie Davis and Mattie Hastings were crying, while Edna Whitely and Mollie Long drew nearer.

"Oh, don't stop," gasped Patty Sands, "please go on, Miss Kate. I'm all excited."

Kate laughed.

"Do let me get my breath, girls. I had no idea it would take me so long."

"There fell no rain that night, but the people as they marched down into the valley thought of nothing but the sacrifice. Probably had it rained they would not have known it. They were silent, thinking with admiration of the wonderful act of heroism that they had just witnessed.

"The next day searching parties started out to seek the bodies of the mother and child, but not a trace could be found.

" 'The Great Spirit has taken them in the flesh,' they said. 'Perhaps He is angry that we allowed it.'

"Everyone grew frightened. None seemed to care to speak. Suddenly a low peal of thunder was heard, then a louder one, after which came a flash of lightning.

" 'A storm!" they cried, 'the sacrifice has not been in vain,' and they fell to their knees.

"It rained as it had never rained before. It fell in sheets. The cattle drank greedily and the water was plentiful. After the third day it grew lighter and the rain slacked. People ventured out of doors, and lo! the valley with the wigwam of Mus-kin-gum had disappeared. In its place, behold! a river. Up and down as far as eye could reach flowed the shining waters. A miracle had been performed, and the wise men came from miles around.

" 'We will call the river O-hi-o,' they said, 'for it is the soul of her who has saved us.'

"And the river spread and grew larger. The braves explored and found that it was too long to measure. It would take days and days to find the end; in fact, they doubted that there could be an end.

"One morning they discovered a smaller river that emptied into the one they had named O-hi-o. That increased in length as well, but with their canoes they could

paddle a hundred miles. They also noticed
a peculiar thing about this smaller river.
Whenever there came a thunder shower the
river would rise and become covered with
whitecaps, and rush madly down like a
torrent until it seemed to fairly leap into
the Ohio; and one wise man—the wisest
of the tribe—said:

" 'Behold, it is little Mus-kin-gum. Can
you not see how the storm affects him?
Was he not so in the flesh? Can you not
see how he seeks his mother's bosom for
shelter?'

"And so the mystery was explained.
From the date of the appearance of the two
rivers everything in that part of the country
prospered. The cattle were second to none.
The fruit was the fairest and most luscious
fruit ever grown, while the crops—corn,
buckwheat, oats, barley and wheat—could
not be excelled."

("Today the fisheries are the finest and
the Grand Reservoir is the largest body of
artificial water in the world—equal in extent to all others in the state. It is well
for you to know that," said Kate, inter-
rupting the story).

"And whenever the Indians prayed to the Great Spirit they would thank him for having sent O-hi-o as a voluntary sacrifice; and each starlight night old Wa-chi-ta and his wife would search among the constellations for their three loved ones. Then they, too, passed into the Happy Hunting Grounds. But with many of the Western tribes the legend remains until today.

"For years to come the little Indian children would say to one another:

" 'It's going to storm. Hear the thunder; see it lighten; let us go down and watch the little Mus-kin-gum get frightened and rush into his mother's arms.' "

"That is the end," said Kate.

"Oh! it is lovely," they all cried, "and we thank you so much."

"You see," she added, "now I am glad that I called this Camp Fire the 'Ohio.' That is our legend, and we can have a little copy made to annex to our book."

Then the Fire Maker came forward and extinguished the dying embers. Each girl arose and kissed the Guardian goodnight, and retired.

CHAPTER XXIV

ETHEL'S FIRST DAY IN CAMP

The girls slept soundly that night and in the morning were awakened by the singing of the birds.

"Oh! how lovely it seems to be here," thought Ethel, as she leaned on her elbow, "instead of being awakened by the toot of an automobile just to lie quietly and harken to the birds." She looked around.

The other cots were occupied by her Cousin Kate, Patty Sands, and Edna Whitely. Kate opened her eyes and sat up.

"Have you been awake long?" she asked sleepily.

"No, Kate, only a few moments. I've been listening to the birds. I thought Aunt Susan's home was peaceful, but even there one could hear the autos."

Kate arose, put on her slippers and wrapper, and sitting on the cot she began to unfasten her long braids.

"It is the most restful place I've ever known," she replied. "But, girls, we're late. Come Patty and Edna."

Patty Sands sat up in bed and rubbed her eyes. Edna snuggled deeper into the depth of her pillow.

"Edna, don't go to sleep. There's the bugle now," and thè clear notes of a bugle came floating into the tent.

"Oh!" said Edna sleepily, "that's Nora Casey blowing. I wish she'd stop; she has the strongest lungs I ever knew."

This morning the breakfast was eaten with a relish. They had oatmeal and cream, ham and eggs, creamed potatoes and coffee. Mollie Long had surprised them with some corn bread that was, as Nora expressed it, "some class."

Their cellar was beside a running brook near the tents. A little waterfall trickled down the rocks with a cheerful sound. Beside the stream was their refrigerator—a large deep hole that had been dug in the ground, and into this, placed in a tightly covered tin bucket, they put their butter, cream, eggs, and meat. It was as cold as ice.   After the pail had been lowered a clean board covered the opening, and on this board they placed a large stone.   But the farmer with whom Mr. Hollister had made arrangement, brought up daily from his place fresh meat, milk, and vegetables, and twice a week pot cheese and buttermilk; so the "Ohio Camp Fires" were in clover. Nothing they ate was stale and everything tasted delicious.

After breakfast was over, Ethel, Nora, and Mollie Long cleared the table, washed the dishes, and tidied up the tent.

CHAPTER XXV

ETHEL'S FIRST LESSON

"Girls," said Kate, after the morning's ceremonies had been performed, "today we will cook our dinner over a real camp fire. Our menu will consist of roasted potatoes, green peas, broiled steak, and a lettuce salad. Sallie Davis is going to make one of her delicious bread puddings, which she will bake in the oil stove, but the rest will be the 'real thing.'"

The girls were delighted.

"Ethel," said Edith Overman, "in August you shall taste our delicious roasted corn. You never ate anything so good in your life. When do you leave for home?"

"August thirtieth," replied the girl. "Do you stay up here until September?"

"Yes," replied Kate. "We leave about the fifth, but on account of you we are going home in August this year."

"Oh, how kind!" said Ethel.

Then Kate began:

"Now my little cousin, you have some work to do today. First, you must learn how to make knots,—the five different styles—but today it shall be a square knot only. You are to tie it five times in sucession without hesitation. You are to read and be able to tell the chief cause of infant mortality in the summer, and to what extent it has been reduced in one American community. That means one city or town. This is your school and you must attend it before you can play. You must learn what to do in the following emergencies: Clothing on fire; person in deep water who can not swim, both in summer and through ice in winter; how to bandage and attend to an open cut; a frosted foot; what to do with a person who has fainted; how to use surgeon's plaster; you must commit to memory a poem of twenty-five lines or more, and you must learn about yourself— what every girl of your age needs to know. You are not to learn all of this in one day, but a little every day. Mollie and Nora, who are proficient in these things, will help teach you. Then you'll learn to cook, swim, and row a boat. We have a lovely lake about a mile from here, and there are boats and canoes to hire. All these, and various other useful things, you are to learn. I want you to be able to win an Elective Honor in some one of the seven crafts. You must wear your beads, but you must win them first. Next week we shall remove the roofs of our tents and sleep in the open. I wish you girls to get a month or two of it. That counts one honor."

Nora, Mollie and Ethel started in. Ethel quickly learned how to tie the knot. Then she began to study "first aid to the injured," and the girls taught her how to adjust a bandage and how to use the plaster.

"It's a shame that ye haven't a real broken bone to work on," laughed Nora.

"Well, that's a nice thing to say," replied Mollie; "suppose you go and cut yourself, Nora Casey, or break your leg."

After studying for a couple of hours the girls declared that Ethel was a promising pupil. She even learned a poem, "The Psalm of Life," by Longfellow.

CHAPTER XXVI

A LOSS AND A DINNER

"Oh! girls," exclaimed Ethel, "I must get my ring. I left it on the box where I washed dishes," and she ran to the kitchen tent, but there was no ring in sight. "I laid it down here and I emptied the water myself," she almost sobbed. "It was a beautiful ring—a diamond cluster. Grandmamma gave it to me. It was her engagement ring."

Kate now came in and they hunted. The girls looked where the water had been thrown but no sign. They swept the tent and searched thoroughly. Mollie Long went back to where Ethel stood half in tears and reported nothing doing.

"Who was with you in the tent?" she asked.

"No one but you and Nora," replied Ethel.

"You remember, Kate," said Ethel,

"it was Grandmamma's engagement ring. I'd have lost anything I own rather than that."

"It's unfortunate," replied Kate, "but perhaps it may turn up."

Poor Ethel took her walk with Patty and Mollie but she was very quiet.

That noon she watched a dinner cooked in the open. Two perpendicular stakes with forked ends had been driven in the ground, while lying horizontally across them was another upon which to hang one or more kettles. Each kettle had an iron hook to place on the cross stake, and from them hung the kettles. A roaring fire had been made. The potatoes were laid in the hot ashes and covered. In one kettle the peas were put. Ethel and Mollie had shelled until their fingers ached.

"Now, girls," said Kate, "someone time those peas. They must not cook longer than three-quarters of an hour, and they must not be covered."

When the salad had been prepared, the bread and butter spread, and the water pitchers filled from the brook it was time to cook the steak.

Four of the girls took forks made from tree branches, placed the steak upon them, and started in. Mollie and Nora in the meanwhile, after draining off nearly all of the water, had put some salt and a little sugar in the peas, adding at the last a large piece of butter, and had placed them in their kettle which stood near the potatoes.

The steak when finished was laid on a large platter and covered plentifully with butter. Then each girl took and opened her potato, and what a potato it was!—so unlike those cooked in an oven. The peas were served in saucers, and the sight of the steak covered with gravy—hot and juicy— made them hungry.

Each sat on the ground with her plate on her lap, and her saucer and glass beside her. They ate up every vestige of food.

"Goodnight!" said Nora. "Shure a dog would starve in this crowd."

After an appetizing salad dressed with a suspicion of garlic and a fine French dressing, came the bread pudding made by Sallie Davis. It was filled with raisins and each girl passed her plate twice.

"Ethel, what do you think of our Camp
Fire dinner?" asked Kate.

"It is simply fine," replied the girl.
"I have never tasted one half so good."

"Poor Ethel, she is unhappy over her
ring," said Edna, and I don't blame her.
Cheer up! it may be found yet," she added.

But Ethel was unhappy, not for the loss
of the ring, but because it had belonged to
old Mrs. Hollister.

"I never should have brought it," she
said to Kate. "I should have left it with
Aunt Susan. I know it was right on the
box when I left the tent, and it's so un-
pleasant," she confided to Kate. "One
suspects everyone."

"Yes, that's the unfortunate part of it,"
replied her cousin. "The innocent suffer
for the guilty; that is, if it has been taken
by anyone, but I have an idea that it may
have been thrown out with the water."

Ethel studied hard every day. She
learned rapidly and one night she received
her first bead. She had learned how to row
a boat and she rowed well. In five days
she had rowed twenty miles, which entitled

her to one honor. Before the next two weeks she had learned how to swim; and she swam one mile in five days. The rule was to swim one mile in six days, but she went one better; so at one of the council fires she received her two beads. As her honors came under "health craft" her beads were red.

Her ceremonial gown had been made for some time. She had worked on it during rainy days, and when she had finished behold! it was perfect.

"Why, you're entitled to another honor. This comes under 'hand craft,' " said Patty.

So now she had won three—two red beads and one of green.

"That's good work," ejaculated Nora Casey. "She'll outstrip us all."

Of course each girl won daily. Some had strings nearly half a yard long. At every council fire the Guardian would distribute them to the girls, but Sallie Davis had the most beads. She was clever and won many for cooking.

About the middle of July there came another set of Camp Fires. They oc-

cupied the woods about half a mile away.
It seemed that the Guardian—a Miss
Andrews—was a schoolmate of Kate Hol-
lister's. They were called the "Columbus
Camp Fires." The girls were friendly and
together they had great sport.

CHAPTER XXVII

A DISCOVERY

One morning Patty and Ethel started for a walk. They were to climb a small mountain. On their way they came across a pocket handkerchief. It was a girl's handkerchief, and on it was the initial "H."

"This isn't Cousin's Kate's I know," said Ethel. "She carried one certain kind with a tiny "H" worked in the corner. This looks like a cheap one that might be purchased for a dime. Whose can it be? Are there any 'H's' in the Columbus Camp Fires?"

They recalled every name—not an "H."

"Then as it isn't Kate's nor mine it must belong to Mattie Hastings."

"Yes," replied Patty. "She often walks up here alone."

"I wish I could get over my feeling of dislike for that girl," said Ethel, "but I can not. It grows on me. I shall be glad to go home to get rid of looking at her. I can never like Nora Casey either, although I have tried very hard. But I positively shrink from that girl. I don't trust her."

"I feel the same, and so do all the girls," replied Patty, "but she seems to have gotten around Miss Hollister. She is invariably hanging on her."

"Cousin Kate is so kind and good-hearted," said Ethel. "She's always ready to make the best of people, but I feel like pulling Mattie Hastings away when I see her around here."

"Look—quick! speak of angels—that was she looking out through those trees," exclaimed Patty. "Now I wonder what she is doing up here and alone. My! but it's warm in the sun, isn't it?" and Patty opened the neck of her waist and removed her hat. "Let's call and see if she answers us."

So Patty Sands called loudly:

"Mattie Hastings—Mattie—we have seen you—don't hide!"

Someone started to run through the brush. They heard a fall and a piercing shriek.

She's tripped,'' said Ethel. "Let's go and see."

Quickly they picked their way over fallen trees and dead leaves until they came to the prostrate body of Mattie whom they so disliked.

"What have you done?" asked Patty. "Have you hurt yourself?"

No answer.

"She's fainted!" ejaculated Ethel. "She's been walking in the sun and exposed to great heat. It's heat exhaustion. See, her face is pale and she isn't entirely unconscious as in a sunstroke. First we must loosen her clothing and let her lie down quietly. I wonder if there is any water about."

"Yes," said Patty, "we passed a watering trough on the road."

While Ethel unbuttoned the girl's waist, Patty ran for water.

"It's lucky I have my drinking cup with me," she called. "I have a long head. I never take a walk without it."

Ethel made no reply. She unhooked the girl's corset. Then when Patty returned, together they lifted her to a shady place. Ethel's face was pale.

"What is the matter?" asked Patty. "You look as though you had seen a ghost."

Ethel pointed to a chain on Mattie's neck. It was a small silver chain, and suspended from it were two diamond rings. One was the small cluster lost by Ethel, while the other was a solitaire. Patty gasped and caught Ethel by the arm.

"That's your ring."

Ethel nodded.

"And the other belongs to Nora Casey. She lost it a few days ago. She didn't want to make a fuss about it on account of you having lost yours, but I think she suspected this girl and determined to get it before she left camp. Isn't it awful?" and Patty shook her head. "You'd better take the chain off before she comes to."

Ethel made no reply but lifted Mattie's head and put the drinking cup to her lips. After a moment the girl took a swallow, then another, until she had taken it all.

"Don't give her any more now," said Ethel. " 'First Aid' says, 'sip slowly in

heat prostrations and give stimulants,' but
we have none."

"Take them off, Ethel," said Patty,
"she might get up and run." But Ethel
only looked.

Suddenly Mattie Hastings opened her
eyes, gazed at the two girls, and at her shirt
waist beside her; then she raised herself and
put her hand to her neck. A scarlet flame
surged across her face.

"You've had a sort of fainting spell,"
said Ethel. "You fell, and the heat and
all made you unconscious for a while. Why
did you run from us when we called?"

With her hands upon her chain the girl
looked like a frightened animal. Something stirred Ethel's pity.

"Don't be frightened," she said, "just
tell us all."

Whereupon Mattie Hastings burst into
tears.

"First hand me my ring," said Ethel,
"and then tell us everything."

The girl tried to unfasten the chain.

"Shall I?", asked Ethel.

Mattie nodded. Then Ethel took the ring.

"To whom does this belong?" she asked.

"Nora," faltered the girl. "Keep it please; I shall never go back. I shall kill myself," she sobbed.

"That's silly," broke in practical Patty.

"Your father—Judge Sands—he will sentence me to prison," she sobbed, "and I did it for Mollie. She's my sister. Her spine is broken and the doctor said she needed food—good nourishing food. She's only eleven, and he told father that with care she might outgrow it, especially if she could get in some Institution for Cripples, where she could have good attention," and the girl threw herself on her face and sobbed brokenly.

"Now, see here," said Ethel, sitting down beside her and lefting her up, while Patty and she supported her back.

"You tell us everything; don't keep even a tiny bit back."

"Yes," broke in Patty, "we're Camp Fire Girls and we must 'Give Service.' Perhaps we can help you if you'll confide in us."

"Before God I will; and I'll tell you all," said Mattie.

CHAPTER XXVIII

MATTIE'S STORY

"My father is a good man. He is kind, hard-working, and gives all of his wages to Mother. Mother has an idea that I am above my associates. She is ambitious for me to go with the rich girls—the girls who have position."

Ethel's heart bounded. Was not her own mother the same?

"I worked in McAllister's store. I earned six dollars a week. Three of it I paid Mother for board. The other three, with what Father gave me, bought my clothes; but even with that I could not dress well enough to go with the girls as she wished me to.

"Her idea was for me to go to church and Sunday School and meet them that way. Then poor little Mollie was knocked down by an automobile and she has never left her bed. They were a party of joy riders,

and oh! I hate to confess it, but I've promised—my mother was one of them. She
had a cousin who was a chauffeur and he
asked her to go. No one but I knew that
she was of the party, for they were so drunk
they never saw that she left them, and to
this day no one knows that it was her
cousin's auto that knocked Mollie down,
for he escaped. Mother came home after
Mollie had been taken to the hospital, and
at that time we all thought that she had
been out spending the evening. When she
found that Mollie was injured for life she
began to take morphine. I alone know her
secret; she never knew that she told it.
For God's sake don't betray me. Every
penny that Father gave her she spent for
that drug, and he thinking that Mollie had
the benefit of it.

"At last I couldn't stand it. I couldn't
see my little sister die for the want of proper
food, nor could I tell Father, and give my
own mother away, for outside of her ambition for me she had been a good mother.
Then Father grew ill and was laid up with
rheumatism. I refused to give Mother

the three dollars for board, but I kept it for expenses. When she demanded, I told her what I knew and threatened to expose her.

"Father grew better and was able to work again, but poor Mollie failed daily. I laid awake night after night. I prayed— for I was a good girl once—for a way to be shown me whereby I could make more than six dollars a week.

"Then in Sunday School I met Miss Hollister. I had heard of these Camp Fire Girls and how many fine things a girl could learn, so that in time she could earn good money. I consulted with Father and he advised me to join; and Mother was delighted, for she saw visions of my being intimate with the 'swell' girls."

Here Mattie put her hands on her breast and Ethel ran to the trough for more water.

"Before we came up here," she continued, "I found a doctor who upon seeing Mollie said that for one hundred and fifty dollars he could put her in a Home where she would have attention and treatment. She could wear braces, and perhaps in time she might grow to be strong and well. But how was I to get it? Father and I together could hardly pay for our food.

"One afternoon just before the store closed a lady dropped her purse. I put my foot over it and stood until she had gone off in her auto. Then when no one was looking I picked it up, put it in my bosom, and went home. In the purse I found forty dollars.

"That was the beginning. After that it came so easy, and Mollie enjoyed the fruit that I brought her. But thirty-five dollars of the money I put in the bank. I took little things from the store and sold them. I pretended that they had been given to me.

"Then I came up here. Oh! I expected to end in prison. I knew that it couldn't go on forever. But I took a chance. I had now nearly seventy-five dollars. One hundred and fifty, or say two hundred, would save Mollie. I kept on. I took a locket from Edith Overman. She's never missed it. It has a large diamond in the center. She's rich and careless. I took that ring from Nora. I've often thought

that Nora suspected me, but she's never
given me away. I've taken money from
each one of you girls. The only one whom
I've not robbed is Miss Kate—God bless
her. I wouldn't take a handkerchief from
her, she's been so kind to me. The rest
have never liked me. You remember since
we came here the time I went home and
spent two days. Well, I went in town and
deposited my money and saw that Mollie
had some comforts in way of food and books.
Then when I came back I began taking the
jewelry. I have now over a hundred dollars
in the bank. I had come up here today to
find a safe place in some tree where until
we went back I could put the two rings and
locket, as I feared that they might be seen
on my neck. When you called and said,
'We've seen you; don't hide,' I thought
that you had discovered that I was a thief
and I started to run and fell over the tree
trunk. I had been pretty warm while
walking up the hill and I guess you were
correct,—it was the heat. That's all,"
she moaned wearily. "You may give me
up. I knew the time would come, but I
had hoped to have had Mollie in a Home

before I was taken," and the girl lay back on the ground shaking with sobs.

Ethel and Patty looked at each other.

"Now see here," said Patty Sands, "Ethel and I are not monsters to eat you up, are we, Ethel?"

"No," replied the girl, "Mattie, I think we may be able to help Mollie."

Mattie sat up.

"What?" she gasped.

"Yes," replied Ethel. "You've done this for her. Now we are not going to betray you, and we are going to help you; but first, you must give back everything that you have taken. Do you remember the name of the lady from whom you took the purse?"

"Yes," replied Mattie. "I have the purse with her card in it."

"Very well; return that by mail. Say if you wish that you found it and regret not sending it before. You needn't sign your name. Then take Nora's ring and put it in her suitcase, after which put Edith's chain in hers. Can you remember the different amounts of money that you have taken from us girls?"

"I took"—and she faltered—"five from you and five from Patty."

"Well, don't try to think now, but go by yourself and if possible remember what you took from each girl and replace it as you are going to replace the jewelry. What-ever you took from the store and sold is a harder matter and you can't recover the goods."

"No," said Mattie.

"How much did you get for them?" asked Patty.

"About twelve dollars," replied the girl.

"You give that to me," said Patty. Mr. McAllister is a great friend of Father's. I will give Father the money and tell him to return it,—that it's from a client—an old employee—who to save a human life and under great temptation took the things, and that she wishes to make restitution. He'll never suspect you, nor will he question Father, for Father has rendered him too many services."

Mattie grasped her by the hand.

"Oh! you are too good to me, Miss Sands. However can I pay you and Miss Ethel?"

"Call me Ethel," said the girl.

"Yes, and me Patty. You are one of us and we are all sisters."

"And now," continued Ethel, "my Aunt Susan, who lives in Akron, is a philanthropist. I've heard her tell of a Cripple's Home there. If your sister is unable to pay she can get her in free. That doctor may slip some of that money he speaks of into his own pocket, and if your sister is under Aunt Susan's wing she'll see that she gets everything she needs, and she'll have the best of care. You can run down every week or so and see her. I'm sure Aunt Susan would make you welcome over night."

Mattie Hastings fell on the ground at the feet of the two girls.

"Oh, my God!" she said, "Are you in earnest?" and she kissed their hands. "Can it be possible that there is about to be made a way for poor Mollie? Are my prayers to be answered?" and she sobbed while the two girls held her in their arms.

"Come on now," said Ethel, "let's go home. You're all tired out. We'll put you to bed. Don't worry, Mattie," she whispered, "we'll attend to everything."

CHAPTER XXIX

MATTIE STARTS AFRESH

Everything was returned as the girls had planned. Mattie went into town, drew out her money, put the forty dollars in the purse and sent it to its owner, as they had suggested.

"Oh, my darling!" she said to Mollie, as she hugged her, "I have great news for you. Come, Mother, and listen."

Then holding each by the hand she related Ethel's proposal.

Mrs. Hastings wept tears of joy while little Mollie laughed.

"Are you sure she'll keep her word?" asked Mrs. Hastings.

"As sure as there's a God in heaven. She's an angel," replied Mattie. "They all are. Oh! Mother, I never knew that there could be such kindness in the world."

Mattie returned, and Ethel and Patty replaced all of the stolen money in the girls' purses save the twelve that was to be given to Judge Sands for McAllister. The jewelry was more difficult, for there was danger of it rolling out of the bags, so Patty suggested putting the ring in a small box and slipping it in Nora's suitcase, and doing the same with the locket belonging to Edith Overman.

The next morning appeared Nora with the ring on her finger, but with never a word. Then rushed out Edith Overman.

"Do you know, I have found my locket and chain. I was awfully worried for I thought I had lost it."

The following day came a reply to Ethel's letter from Aunt Susan. This was the extract pertaining to the Home:

"Yes, my dear, I can get the little girl in the Cripples' School free—not 'Home.' In this place she'll have the best of medical attendance. I am one of the managers. She will be taught to sew and make lovely things besides having good nourishing food every day. Her sister is welcome to stay with us whenever she cares to come. The little girl will probably come out cured, and it will not cost her a penny. Even her clothes will be furnished. Let me know when to expect them. I enclose your mother's letter."

Mattie cried with joy.

"What is it?" the girls asked, and she told them.

Judge Sands had seen Mr. McAllister who took the money without a comment save:

"Well, Judge, when a thing happens like this it sort of restores one's faith in human nature, doesn't it?"

And Mattie was a happy girl.

"Really," said Ethel to her cousin and Patty, "Mattie's eyes have grown wider apart."

"No, it's because you like her and she seems different to you."

Mrs. Hollister wrote:

"My dearest girl:

"I hope you have made only desirable acquaintances and that you will forget the Camp Fire Girls, at least this winter. You will be seventeen soon and I shall give you a debutante's party. I have saved considerable money during your absence."

Ethel didn't answer the letter at once.

One day came up the hill the buckboard holding three men. The girls saw it from a distance, and there was some excitement. As it drew nearer three shouts went up. There was Tom Harper, Uncle John, and Judge Sands.

Ethel almost wept on Tom's shoulder, and she was well hugged by Uncle John.

That was the day that they had their great Camp Fire dinner—when they soaked the corn for an hour in water before roasting it. Then tying a string to each ear they laid it in the glowing fire and ate it with melted butter and salt. The Judge and Uncle John ate three ears apiece, besides the potatoes, chicken, and steamed berry pudding made by Patty, his daughter.

"Say, John and Tom," he said, "we'd better come up here and board. No wonder these girls like to get away from town."

And Mattie was introduced to the Judge by Patty.

"Papa," she said, "this is Mattie Hastings, and when I was ill she sat up the entire night taking care of me and putting fresh flax-seed poultices on my chest."

And the Judge thanked her so sincerely that she nearly burst into tears.

"And your father?" he asked, "how is he?   I need a man just like him in my office. I've met him, and Miss Mattie, there's one thing I've always liked about him,—he has a face that anyone could trust.   I shall go and see him on my return."

Then Mattie was not afraid to weep with joy as she clasped the Judge's hand and thanked him sincerely.

"Well, girls," said Uncle John, "we'll be looking for you next week—hey?"

"Yes," replied Kate, "and, Father, I'd like to have Aunt Susan come up before we leave.   She'd enjoy it."

"Oh! yes," fairly shouted Ethel.   "Do bring her, Tom."

CHAPTER XXX

AUNT SUSAN COMES

So the day Aunt Susan came, everyone was on the qui vive, and a warmer welcome was never extended to an old lady. She was shown everything. She had a real Camp Fire dinner and enjoyed it.

She took Mattie one side and told her of the wonderful improvement in little Mollie, which made Mattie's heart beat high with joy.

When she was introduced to Honora the girl made such quaint remarks that Aunt Susan laughed merrily.

"Isn't it funny?" said Ethel; "that's the only girl in Camp that I don't care for."

"Ethel," replied her aunt, "perhaps, you don't know her as she really is."

"Perhaps," responded Ethel slowly, thinking of Mattie.

The evening that Aunt Susan stayed

Ethel was advanced from a Wood Gatherer to a Fire Maker. She stood up in her ceremonial dress with her pretty hair hanging, and bound with a band of beads called her "ceremonial band," and she repeated the Fire Maker's song.

New honors were awarded. They had songs and toasts, one of which was "Aunt Susan," after which the girls repeated in unison:

"Burn, fire, burn; flicker, flicker, flame, etc."

Then, extinguishing the fire, they retired for the night.

The next morning the Camp broke up. Ethel bade them all an affectionate farewell. She even kissed Honora. There seemed to be a spirit of good will among all of the girls.

"Be sure and come back next summer, Ethel," was heard on every side.

And Mattie, taking her apart from the rest, said:

"You have saved me from a fate worse than death. I was going the downward path, and you and Patty lifted me out of the mud. I shall pray for you every night. Don't forget me."

"No, I shall not," replied Ethel, kissing her affectionately, "and you promise to go and see little Mollie and write me all about her, won't you?"

CHAPTER XXXI

After spending the night at Uncle John's, Aunt Susan and Ethel left for Akron.

"Oh! what a lovely summer I've had," said Ethel, "and how much I've learned being a Camp Fire Girl; and I owe it all to you, Aunt Susan."

The next week Mr. Hollister came to take the girl home—and how he had missed her!

They spent the day with Uncle John. He and her father were like boys again.

"You must come here next year, Archibald," said John, "and go up to Camp and see the way these girls keep house. It's a revelation. What the women are coming to! I don't believe there'll be any room on earth for us men after a while."

Ethel's eyes were blinded with tears as she kissed her dear ones goodbye, and Mattie Hastings with Patty Sands came way to Akron to see her off, Mattie bringing

the loveliest pin-cushion made for her by
her sister Mollie.

One night Ethel and Mrs. Hollister had a
serious talk. Grandmother made Archibald go and listen at the door, as Bella's
voice could be heard throughout the house.

When Ethel left her mother she went
directly up to her room, but Mrs. Hollister
said to Grandmother:

"This is your work and your sister's as
well. Ethel is a changed girl and refused
to obey me. She's going to take up low
settlement work and belong to that Camp
Fire business this winter, and she almost
refuses to go into society at all. But for
the fact that some of our best girls are Camp
Fires I should positively forbid it. She is
not yet of age, and I still have some author-
ity over her, after all my slaving for her
and sacrifices. Now she openly defies me."

"No, Mamma," cried Ethel, coming
down stairs and putting her arm around her
mother, "I only object to sailing under
false colors. All of our life has been sham—
sham—and make believe, and I can not
see Papa growing older and more bent

every day, when he should be young looking and happy. And I know that it's
worry over getting the money for me that
I may make a show for people to think me
wealthy. And when Aunt Susan came here
you told everyone that I was to be her heiress.
Why, Mamma, she is poorer than we are.
Every penny of her money was lost four
years ago, and Tom Harper—her adopted
son—supports her. Then there's dear Uncle John. He's nearly five years older than
Papa and he looks ten years younger.
Why? Because he has nothing to worry
him. And when I see the lines and wrinkles
coming into your pretty face I think it's
all for me, and I've decided to give it up.
I shall still go out with the friends who care
for me, but they must know me as I am;
and next summer I want you to come with
me to Camp. You are so clever and can
teach the girls so much about sewing and
dressmaking.

"Mamma dear, let's turn over a new
leaf. Let's give up all sham and be happy.
Then we can tell who are our true friends
and they'll be all we need."

Here Ethel put her arms around her
mother who at once burst into tears, sobbing:

"And I wanted you to make a g-good
m-match."

"Never mind," laughed Ethel. "Who
knows? I may marry better than ever.
Cheer up, Mamma dear," and from that
hour the mother and daughter changed
places.

And Grandmother Hollister whispered
to her son:

"Behold! a miracle."

THE BLUE DWARFS:

AN ADVENTURE IN THURINGEN

"And then on the top of the Caldon Low
There was no one left but me."
MARY HOWITT.

"I LIKED the blue dwarfs the best—far, far the best of anything," said Olive.

"'The blue dwarfs!'" repeated Rex. "What *do* you mean? Why can't you say what you mean plainly? Girls have such a stupid way of talking!"

"What can be plainer than *the blue dwarfs*?" said Olive rather snappishly, though, it must be allowed, with some reason. "We were talking about the things we liked best at the china place. *You* said the stags' heads and the inkstands, and *I* say the blue dwarfs."

"But I didn't see any dwarfs," persisted Rex

"Well, I can't help it if you didn't. You had just as much chance of seeing them as I had. They

were in a corner by themselves—little figures about
two inches high, all with blue coats on. There
were about twelve of them, all different, but all
little dwarfs or gnomes. One was sitting on a
barrel, one was turning head-over-heels, one was
cuddling his knees—all funny ways like that. Oh,
they were lovely!"

"I wish I had seen them better," said Rex regret-
fully. "I do remember seeing a tray full of little
blue-looking dolls, but I didn't notice what they
were."

Olive did not at once answer. Her eyes were
fixed on something she saw passing before the window. It was a very, very little man. He was not
exactly hump-backed, but his figure was somewhat
deformed, and he was so small that but for the
sight of his rather wizened old face one could
hardly have believed he was a full-grown man.
His eyes were bright and beady-looking, like those
of a good-natured little weasel, if there be such a
thing, and his face lighted up with a smile as he
caught sight of the two, to him, strange-looking
children at the open window of the little village
inn.

"Guten Tag," he said, nodding to them; and
"Guten Tag," replied the children, as they had
learnt to do by this time to everybody they met

For in these remote villages it would be thought the greatest breach of courtesy to pass any one without this friendly greeting.

Rex drew a long breath when the dwarf had passed.

"Olive——" he began, but Olive interrupted him.

"Rex," she said eagerly, "that's *exactly* like them—like the blue dwarfs, I mean. Only, of course, their faces were prettier—nice little china faces, rather crumply looking, but quite nice; and then their coats were such a pretty nice blue. I think," she went on consideringly—"I think, if I had that little man and washed his face *very* well, and got him a bright blue coat, he would look just like one of the blue dwarfs grown big."

Rex looked at Olive with a queer expression.

"Olive," he said in rather an awe-struck tone; "Olive, do you think perhaps they're *real*? Do you think perhaps somewhere in this country—in those queer dark woods, perhaps—that there are real blue dwarfs, and that somebody must have seen them and made the little china ones like them? Perhaps," and his voice dropped and grew still more solemn; "*perhaps*, Olive, that little man's one of them, and they may have to take off their blue coats when they're walking about. Do you know, I think it's a little, just a very little frightening? Don't you, Olive?"

"No, of course I don't," said Olive, and, to do
her justice, her rather sharp answer was meant as
much to reassure her little brother as to express
any feeling of impatience. Rex was quite a little
fellow, only eight, and Olive, who was nearly
twelve, remembered that when she was as little as
that, she used sometimes to feel frightened about
things which she now couldn't see anything the
least frightening in. And she remembered how
once or twice some of her big cousins had laughed
at her, and amused themselves by telling her all
sorts of nonsense, which still seemed terrible to her
when she was alone in her room in the dark at
night. "Of course there's nothing frightening in
it," she said. "It would be rather a funny idea, I
think. Of course it can't be, you know, Rex.
There are no dwarfs, and gnomes, and fairies now."

"But that little man was a dwarf," said Rex.

Yes, but a dwarf needn't be a fairy sort of person,"
explained Olive. "He's just a common little man,
only he's never grown as big as other people. Perhaps he had a bad fall when he was a baby—that
might stop his growing."

"Would it?" said Rex. "I didn't know that. I
hope I hadn't a bad fall when I was a baby. Everybody says I'm very small for my age." And Rex
looked with concern at his short but sturdy legs.

Olive laughed outright.

"Oh, Rex, what a funny boy you are! No, certainly, you are not a dwarf. You're as straight and strong as you can be."

"Well, but," said Rex, returning to the first subject, "I do think it's very queer about that little dwarf man coming up the street just as you were telling me about the blue dwarfs. And he *did* look at us in a funny way, Olive, whatever you say, just as if he had heard what we were talking about."

"All the people look at us in a funny way here," said Olive. "We must look very queer to them. Your sailor suit, Rex, and my 'Bolero' hat must look to them quite as queer as the women's purple skirts, with bright green aprons, look to us."

"Or the bullock-carts," said Rex. Do you remember how queer we thought them at first? *Now* we've got quite used to seeing queer things, haven't we, Olive, Oh! now, do look there—at the top of the street—there Olive, did you *ever* see such a load as that woman is carrying in the basket on her back? Why, it's as big as a house!"

He seemed to have forgotten about the dwarfs, and Olive was rather glad of it. These two children were travelling with their uncle and aunt in a rather out-of-the-way part of Germany. Out-of-the-way, that is to say, to most of the regular summer tourists from other countries, who prefer going where they are more sure of finding the comforts and luxuries they are accustomed to at home. But it was by no means out-of-the-way in the sense of being dull or deserted. It is a very busy part of the world indeed. You would be amazed if I were to tell you some of the beautiful things that are made in these bare homely little German cottages. For all about in the neighborhood there are great manufactories and warehouses for china and glass, and many other things; and some parts of the work are done by the people at home in their own houses. The morning of the day of which I am telling you had been spent by the children and their friends in visiting a very large china manufactory, and their heads were full of the pretty and wonderful things they had seen.

And now they were waiting in the best parlor of the village inn while their uncle arranged about a carriage to take them all on to the small town where they were to stay a few days. Their aunt was tired, and was resting a little on the sofa, and they had planted themselves on the broad window-sill, and were looking out with amusement at all that passed.

"What have you two been chattering about all this time?" said their aunt, suddenly looking up. "I think I must have been asleep a little, but I have heard your voices going on like two birds twittering."

"Have we disturbed you, Auntie?" asked Olive, with concern.

"Oh no, not a bit; but come here and tell me what you have been talking about."

Instantly Rex's mind went back to the dwarfs.

"Auntie," he said seriously, "perhaps you can tell me better than Olive can. Are there really countries of dwarfs, and are they a kind of fairies, Auntie?"

Auntie looked rather puzzled.

"Dwarfs, Rex?" she said; "countries of dwarfs? How do you mean?"

Olive hastened to explain. Auntie was very much amused.

"Certainly," she said, "we have already seen so many strange things in our travels that it is better not to be too sure what we may not see. But any way, Rex, you may be quite easy in your mind, that if ever you come across any of the dwarfs, you will find them very good-natured and amiable, only you must be very respectful—always say 'Sir,' or 'My lord,' or something like that to them, and bow a great deal. And you must never seem to think anything they do the least odd, not even if they propose to you to walk on your head, or to eat roast fir-cones for dinner, for instance."

Auntie was quite young—not so very much older, than Olive—and very merry. Olive's rather "grown-up" tones and manners used sometimes to tempt her to make fun of the little girl, which, to tell the truth, Olive did not always take quite in good part. And it must for Olive be allowed, that Auntie did sometimes allow her spirits and love of fun to run away with her a little too far, just like pretty unruly ponies, excited by the fresh air and sunshine, who toss their heads and gallop off. It is great fun at first and very nice to see, but one is sometimes afraid they may do some mischief on the way—without meaning it, of course; and, besides, it is not always so easy to pull them up as it was to start them.

Just as Auntie finished speaking the door opened and their uncle came in. He was Auntie's elder brother—a good deal older—and very kind and sensible. At once all thoughts of the dwarfs or what Auntie had been saying danced out of Rex's curly head. Like a true boy he flew off to his uncle, besieging him with questions as to what sort of a carriage they were to go on in—*was* it an ox-cart; oh, mightn't they *for once* go in an ox-cart? and might he—oh, might he sit beside the driver in front?

His uncle laughed and replied to his questions,

but Olive stayed beside the sofa, staring gravely at
her aunt.

"Auntie," she said, "you're not *in earnest*, are
you, about there being really a country of dwarfs?"

Olive was twelve. Perhaps you will think her
very silly to have imagined for a moment that her
aunt's joke could be anything but a joke, especially
as she had been so sensible about not letting Rex
get anything into his head which could frighten
him. But I am not sure that she was so very silly
after all. She had read in her geography about
the Lapps and Finns, the tiny little men of the
north, whom one might very well describe as
dwarfs; there might be dwarfs in these stange
Thuringian forests, which were little spoken of in
geography books; Auntie knew more of such things
than she did, for she had traveled in this country
before. Then with her own eyes Olive had seen a
dwarf, and though she had said to Rex that he
was just an odd dwarf by himself as it were, not
one of a race, how could she tell but what he might
be one of a number of such queer little people?
And even the blue dwarfs themselves—the little
figures in the china manufactory—rather went to
prove it than not.

"They may have taken the idea of dwarfs from
the real ones, as Rex said," thought Olive. "Any

way I shall look well about me if we go through
any of these forests again. They must live in the
forests, for Auntie said they eat roast fir-cones for
dinner."

All these thoughts were crowding through her
mind as she stared up into Auntie's face and asked
solemnly—

"Auntie, were you in earnest?"

Auntie's blue eyes sparkled.

"In earnest, Olive?" she said. "Of course!
Why shouldn't I be in earnest? But come, quick,
we must get our things together. Your uncle must
have got a carriage."

"Yes," said he, "I have. *Not* an ox-cart, Rex.
I'm sorry for your sake, but for no one else's; for I
don't think there would be much left of us by the
end of the journey if we were to be jogged along the
forest roads in an ox-cart. No! I have got quite
a respectable vehicle; but we must stop an hour or
two on the way, to rest the horses and give them a
feed, otherwise we could not get through to-night."

"Where shall we stop?" said Auntie, as with the
bundles of shawls and bags they followed the children's uncle to the door.

"There is a little place in the forest, where they
can look after the horses," said he; "and I daresay
we can get some coffee there for ourselves, if we

want it. It is a pretty little nook. I remember it long ago, and I shall be glad to see it again."

Olive had pricked up her ears. "A little place in the forest!" she said to herself; "that may be near where the dwarfs live; it is most likely not far from here, because of the one we saw." She would have liked to ask her uncle about it, but something in the look of her aunt's eyes kept her from doing so.

"Perhaps she *was* joking," thought Olive to herself. "But perhaps she doesn't know; *she* didn't see the real dwarf. It would be rather nice if I did find them, *then* Auntie couldn't laugh at me any more."

They were soon comfortably settled in the carriage, and set off. The first part of the drive was not particularly interesting; and it was so hot, though already afternoon, that they were all— Olive especially, you may be sure—delighted to exchange the open country for the pleasant shade of a grand pine forest, through which their road now lay.

"Is it a very large forest, Uncle?" said Olive.

"Yes, very large," he replied rather sleepily, to tell the truth; for both he and Auntie had been nodding a little, and Rex had once or twice been fairly asleep. But Olive's imagination was far too hard at work to let her sleep.

"The largest in Europe?" she went on, without giving much thought to poor Uncle's sleepiness.

"Oh, yes, by far," he replied, for he had not heard clearly what she said, and fancied it was "the largest hereabouts."

"Dear me!" thought Olive, looking round her with awe and satisfaction. "If there are dwarfs anywhere, then it must be here."

And she was just beginning another. "And please, Uncle, is——?" when her aunt looked up and said lazily—

"Oh, my dear child, do be quiet! Can't you go to sleep yourself a little? We shall have more than enough of the forest before we are out of it." Which offended Olive so much that she relapsed into silence.

Auntie was a truer prophet than she knew, for when she got to the little hamlet in the wood, where they were to rest, something proved to be wrong with one of the horse's shoes—*so* wrong, indeed, that after a prolonged examination, at which all the inhabitants turned out to assist, it was decided that the horse must be re-shod before he could go any farther; and this made it impossible for the party who had come in the carriage to go any farther either. For the nearest smithy was two miles off; the horse must be led there and back by the driver, which would take at least two, if not three, hours. It was now past six, and they had come barely half way. The driver shook his head, and said he would not like to go on to the town till morning. The horse had pricked his foot; it might cause inflammation to drive him farther without a rest, and the carriage was far too heavy for the other horse alone, which had suddenly struck the children's uncle as a brilliant idea.

"There would be no difficulty about the harness-ing, any way," he said to Auntie, laughing, "for all the vehicles hereabouts drawn by one horse have the animal at one side of a pole, instead of between shafts."

But Auntie thought it better to give in.

"It really doesn't much matter," she said; "we can stay here well enough. There are two bed-rooms, and no doubt they can give us something to eat—beer and sausages, and brown bread, any way."

And so it was settled, greatly to Olive's satis-faction; it would give her capital opportunities for a dwarf hunt, though as to this she kept her own counsel.

The landlady of the little post-house where they had stopped was accustomed to occasional visits of this kind from benighted or distressed travellers. She thought nothing of turning her two daughters out of their bedroom, which, it must be owned, was very clean, for Auntie and Olive, and a second room on the ground-floor was prepared for Rex and his uncle. She had coffee ready in five minutes, and promised them a comfortable supper before bedtime. Altogether, everything seemed very satisfactory, and when they felt a little re, freshed, Auntie proposed a walk—"a good long walk," she said, "would do us good. And the land-lady says we get out of the forest up there behind the house, where the ground rises, and that there is a lovely view. It will be rather a climb, but it isn't more than three-quarters of an hour from here, and we have not walked all day."

Uncle thought it a good idea, and Rex was ready to start at once; but Olive looked less pleased.

"Don't you want to come, Olive?" said Auntie. "Are you tired? You didn't take a nap like the rest of us."

"I am a little tired," said Olive, which was true in one sense, though not in another, for she was quite fit for a walk. It struck her that her excuse was not quite an honest one, so she added, "If you don't mind, I would rather stay about here. I don't mind being alone, and I have my book. And I do so like the forest."

"Very well," said her uncle; "only don't lose yourself. She is perfectly safe," he added, turning to her aunt; "there are neither wolves, nor bears, nor robbers nowadays, in these peaceful forests."

So the three set off, leaving Olive to her own devices. She waited till they were out of sight, then she made her preparations.

"I'd better take my purse," she said to herself, "in case I meet the dwarfs. Auntie told me to be very polite, and perhaps they would like some of these tiny pieces; they just look as if they were meant for them." So she chose out a few one-pfennig copper coins, which are much smaller than our farthings, and one or two silver pieces, worth about twopence-halfpenny each, still smaller. Then she put in her pocket half a slice of the brown bread they had had with their coffee, and arming herself, more for appearance sake than anything else, with her parasol and the book she had with her in her travelling bag, she set off on her solitary ramble.

It was still hot—though the forest trees made a pleasant shade. Olive walked some way, farther and farther—as far as she could make out—into the heart of the forest, but in her inexperience she took no sort of care to notice the way she went, or to make for herself any kind of landmarks. She just wandered on and on, tempted first by some mysterious little path, and then by another, her mind full of the idea of the discoveries she was perhaps about to make. Now and then a squirrel darted across from one tree to another, disappearing among the branches almost before Olive could be sure she had seen it, or some wild wood birds, less familiar to the little foreigner, would startle her with a shrill, strange note. There were her end there lovely flowers growing among the moss, and more than once she heard the sound of not far off trickling water. It was all strangely beautiful, and she would greatly have enjoyed and admired it had not her mind been so full of the queer fascinating idea of the blue dwarfs.

At last—she had wandered about for some time —Olive began to feel tired.

"I may as well sit down a little," she thought; "I have lots of time to get back. This seems the very heart of the forest. They are just as likely to be seen here as anywhere else."

So Olive ensconced herself in a comfortable corner, her back against the root of a tree, which seemed hollowed out on purpose to serve as an arm-chair. She thought at first she would read a little, but the light was already slightly waning, and the tree shadows made it still fainter. Be-

sides, Olive had plenty to think of—she did not re-
quire any amusement. Queer little noises now
and then made themselves heard—once or twice it
really sounded as if small feet were pattering
along, or as if shrill little voices were laughing in
the distance; and with each sound Olive's heart
beat faster with excitement—not with fear.

"If I sit very still," she thought, "who knows
what I may see? Of course, it would be much nicer
and prettier if the dwarfs were quite tiny—not like
the little man we saw in the street at that place—
I forget the name—for he was not pretty at all—
but like the dwarfs at the manufactory. But that,
I suppose, is impossible, for they would be really
like fairies. But they might be something between:
not so big as the little man, and yet bigger than
the blue dwarfs."

And then Olive grew a little confused in trying
to settle in her mind how big, or how small rather,
it was possible or impossible for a nation of dwarfs
to be. She thought it over till she hardly seemed
sure what she was trying to decide. She kept saying to herself, "Any way, they could not but be a
good deal bigger than my thumb! What does
that mean? Perhaps it means more in German
measures than in English, perhaps——"

But what was that that suddenly hit her on the

nose? Olive looked up, a very little inclined to be offended; it is not a pleasant thing to be hit on the nose; could it be Rex come behind her suddenly, and playing her a trick? Just as she was thinking this, a second smart tap on the nose startled her still more, and this time there was no mistake about it; it came from above, and it was a fir-cone! Had it come of itself? Somehow the words, "Roast fir-cones for dinner," kept running in her head, and she took up the fir-cone in her fingers to examine it, but quickly dropped it again for it was as hot as a coal.

"It has a very roasty smell," thought Olive; "where can it have come from?"

And hardly had she asked herself the question, when a sudden noise all round her made her again look up. They were sliding down the branches of the tree in all directions. At first, to her dazzled eyes, they seemed a whole army, but as they touched the ground one by one, and she was able to distinguish them better, she saw that after all there were not so *very* many. One, two, three, she began quickly counting to herself, not aloud, of course—that would not have been polite—one, two, three, up to twelve, then thirteen, fourteen, and so on up to—yes, there were just twenty-four of them.

"Two of each," said Olive to herself; "a double set of the blue dwarfs."

For they were the blue dwarfs, and no mistake! Two of each, as Olive had seen at once. And immediately they settled themselves in twos—two squatted on the ground embracing their knees, two strode across a barrel which they had somehow or other brought with them, two began turning head-over-heels, two knelt down with their heads and queer little grinning faces looking over their shoulders, twos and twos of them in every funny position you could imagine, all arranged on the mossy ground in front of where Olive sat, and all dressed in the same bright blue coats as the toy dwarfs at the china manufactory.

Olive sat still and looked at them. Somehow she did not feel surprised.

"How big are they?" she said to herself. "Bigger than my thumb? Oh yes, a good deal. I should think they are about as tall as my arm would be if it was standing on the ground. I should think they would come up above my knee. I should like to stand up and measure, but perhaps it is better for me not to speak to them till they speak to me."

She had not long to wait. In another moment two little blue figures separated themselves from the crowd, and made their way up to her. But when they were close to her feet they gave a sudden jump in the air, and came down, not on their feet, but on their heads! And then again some of her aunt's words came back to her, "If they should ask you to stand on your head, for instance."

"Dear me," thought Olive, "how did Auntie know so much about them? But I do hope they won't ask me to stand on *my* head."

Her fears were somewhat relieved when the dwarfs gave another spring and came down this time in a respectable manner on their feet. Then, with a good many bows and flourishes, they began a speech.

"We are afraid," said the first.

"That the fir-cones," said the second.

"Were rather underdone," finished up the first.

Olive really did not know what to say. She was dreadfully afraid that it would seem so very rude of her not even to have *tasted* the cones. But naturally she had not had the slightest idea that they had been intended for her to eat.

"I am very sorry," she said, "Mr. ——, sir! my lord! I beg your pardon. I don't quite know what I should call you."

"With all respect," said the first.

"And considering the circumstances," went on the second.

Then, just as Olive supposed they were going to

tell her their names, they stopped short and looked at her.

"I beg your pardon," she began again, after waiting a minute or two to see if they had nothing else to say; "I don't quite understand."

"Nor do we," they replied promptly, speaking for the first time both together.

"Do you mean you don't know what *my* name is?" said she. "It's Olive, *Olive!* for the dwarfs stood staring as if they had not heard her. "OLIVE!" she repeated for the third time.

"Green?" asked the first.

"No!" said Olive. "Of course not! *Green* is a very common name—at least——"

"But you called us 'blue,'" said the second; and it really was a relief to hear him finish a sentence comfortably by himself, only Olive felt very puzzled by what he said.

"How do you know?" she said. "How could you tell I called you the blue dwarfs?" and then another thought suddenly struck her. How very odd it was that the dwarf spoke such good English! "I thought you were German," she said.

"How very amusing!" said the dwarfs, this time again speaking together.

Olive could not see that it was very amusing, but she was afraid of saying so, for fear it should be rude.

"And about the fir-cones," went on the first dwarf. "It is distressing to think they were so underdone. But we have come, all of us," waving his hand in the direction of the others, "to invite you to supper in our village. There you will find them done to perfection."

"Olive felt more and more uncomfortable.

"You are very kind," she said. "I should like to come very much if it isn't too far; but I am afraid I couldn't eat any supper. Indeed, I'm not hungry." And then a bright thought struck her.

"See here," she went on, drawing the half slice of bread out of her pocket, "I had to put this in my pocket, for I couldn't finish it at our afternoon coffee."

The two dwarfs came close and examined the piece of bread with the greatest attention. They pinched and smelt it, and one of them put out his queer little pointed tongue and licked it.

"Not good!" he said, looking up at Olive and rolling about his eyes in a very queer way.

"I don't know," said Olive; I don't think it can be bad. It is the regular bread of the country. I should have thought you would be accustomed to it, as you live here."

The two dwarfs took no notice of what she said, but suddenly turned round, and standing with their backs to Olive called out shrilly, "Guten Tag." Immediately all the other dwarfs replied in the same tone and the same words, and to Olive's great surprise they all began to move towards her, but without altering their attitudes—those on the barrel rolled towards her without getting off it; the two who were hugging their knees continued to hug them, while they came on by means of jerking themselves; the turning head-over-heels ones span along like wheels, and so on till the whole assemblage were at her feet. Then she saw unfolded before her, hanging on the branches of the tree, a large mantle, just the shape of her aunt's traveling dust-cloak, which she always spread over Olive in a carriage, only, instead of being drab or fawn-colored, it was, like the dwarfs' jackets, bright blue. And without any one telling her, Olive seemed to know of herself that she was to put it on.

She got up and reached the cloak easily; it seemed to put itself on, and Olive felt very happy and triumphant as she said to herself, "Now I'm really going to have some adventures."

The dwarfs marched—no, one cannot really call it marching, for they had about a dozen different ways of proceeding—they moved on, and Olive in the middle, her blue cloak floating majestically on her shoulders. No one spoke a word. It grew darker and darker among the trees, but Olive did not feel frightened. On they went, until at last she saw twinkling before them a very small but bright blue light. It looked scarcely larger than the lamp of a glowworm, but it shone out very distinct in the darkness. Immediately they saw it the dwarfs set up a shout, and as it died away, to Olive's surprise, they began to sing. And what do you think they sang? Olive at first could hardly believe her ears as they listened to the thoroughly English song of "Home, Sweet Home." And the queerest thing was that they sang it very prettily, and that it sounded exactly like her annt's voice! And though they were walking close beside her, their voices when they left off singing did not so much seem to stop as to move off—to die away into the distance —which struck Olive as very odd.

They had now arrived at the trunk of a large tree, half way up which hung the little lamp—at least Olive supposed it must be a lamp—from which came the bright blue light.

"Here we are," said one of the dwarfs, she did not see which, "at the entrance to our village." And thereupon all the dwarfs began climbing up the tree, swarming about it like a hive of bees, till they got some way up, when one after another they suddenly disappeared. Olive could see all they did by the blue light. She was beginning to wonder if she would be left standing there alone, when a shout made her look up, and she saw two dwarfs standing on a branch holding a rope ladder, which they had just thrown down, and making signs to her to mount up by it. It was quite easy; up went Olive, step by step, and when she reached the place where the two dwarfs were standing, she saw how it was that they had all disappeared. The tree trunk was hollow, and there were steps cut in it like a stair, down which the dwarfs signed to her that she was to go. She did not need to be twice told, so eager was she to see what was to come. The stair was rather difficult for her to get down without falling, for the steps were too small, being intended for the dwarfs, but Olive managed pretty well, only slipping now and then. The stair seemed very long, and as she went farther it grew darker, till at last it was quite dark, by which time, fortunately, however, she felt herself again on level ground, and after waiting half a minute a door seemed to open, and she found herself standing outside the tree stair, with the prettiest sight before her eyes that she had ever seen or even imagined.

It was the dwarf village. Rows and rows of tiny houses—none of them more than about twice as high as Olive herself, for that was quite big enough for a dwarf cottage, each with a sweet little garden in front, like what one sees in English villages, though the houses themselves were like Swiss chalets. It was not dark down here; there was a soft light about as bright as we have it at summer twilight, and besides this, each little house had a twinkling blue light hanging above the front door like a sign post. And at the door of each cottage stood one of the dwarfs, with a little dwarf wife beside him; only, instead of blue, each little woman was dressed in brown, so that they were rather less showy than their husbands. They all began bowing as Olive appeared, and all the little women courtesying, and Olive seemed to understand without being told, that she was to walk up the village street to see all there was to be seen. So on she marched, her blue cloak floating about her, so that sometimes it reached the roofs of the houses on each side at the same time.

Olive felt herself rather clumsy. Her feet, which in general, she was accustomed to consider rather neat, and by no means too large for her age, seemed such great awkward things. If she had put one of them in at the window of a dwarf house, it would have knocked everything out of its place.

"Dear me!" thought Olive, "I had no idea *I* could

seem clumsy! I feel like a great ploughman. I wish I were not so big."

"Yes," said a voice beside her, "it has its disadvantages;" and Olive, looking down to see who spoke—she had to look down for everything—caught sight of one of the two dwarfs with whom she had first spoken. She felt a little ruffled. She did not like this trick of the dwarf hearing what she thought before she said it.

"Everything has its disadvantages," she replied.

"Don't you find yourself very inconveniently small when you are up in *our* world?"

"Exactly so," said the dwarf; but he did not seem the least put out.

"They are certainly very good-tempered," said Olive to herself. Then suddenly a thought struck her.

"Your village is very neat and pretty," she said; "though, perhaps—I don't mean to be rude, not on any account——"

"No,," interrupted the dwarf; "Auntie told you on no account to be rude."

"Auntie!" repeated Olive, in astonishment; "she is not *your* auntie!"

"On no account," said the dwarf, in the same calm tone, but without seeming to take in that Olive meant to reprove him.

"It's no use trying to make them understand," said Olive to herself.

"Not the least," said the dwarf; at which Olive felt so provoked that she could have stamped her feet with irritation. But as *thinking* crossly seemed in this country to be quite as bad as *speaking* crossly, she had to try to swallow down her vexation as well as she could.

"I was going to say," she went on quietly, "that to my taste the village would be prettier if there was a little variety. Not all the houses just the same, you know. And all of *you* are so like each other, and all your little brown wives too. Are there no *children* dwarfs?"

"Doubtless. Any quantity," was the answer.

"Then where are they all?" said Olive. "Are they all asleep?" She put the last question rather sarcastically, but the sarcasm seemed to be lost on the little man.

"Yes, all asleep," he replied; "all asleep, and dreaming. Children are very fond of dreaming," he went on, looking up at Olive with such a queer expression, and such a queer tone in his voice, too, that Olive got a queer feeling herself, as if he meant more than his words actually said. Could he mean to hint that *she* was dreaming? But a remark from the dwarf distracted her thoughts.

"Supper is ready," he said. "They are all waiting." And turning round, Olive saw before her a
cottage a good deal larger than the others; in
fact, it was almost high enough for her, with considerable stooping, to get in at the door. And
through the windows she saw a long table neatly
covered with a bright blue table-cloth, and spread
with numbers of tiny plates, and beside each plate
a knife and fork and a little blue glass cup. Two
great dishes stood on the table, one at each end.
Steam was rising from each, and a delicious smell
came out through the open windows.

"I did not know I was so hungry," thought
Olive; "but I do *hope* it isn't fir-cones."

"Yes," said the dwarf; "they'll be better done
this time."

Then he gave a sort of sharp, sudden cry or
whistle, and immediately all the dwarfs of the village appeared as if by magic, and began hurrying
into the house, but as soon as they were in the
middle of the passage they fell back at each side,
leaving a clear space in the middle.

"For you," said the first dwarf, bowing politely.

"Do you always have supper here altogether
like that?" said Olive. "How funny!"

"Not at all," said the dwarf; "it's a table
d'hote. Be so good as to take your place."

Olive bent her head cautiously in preparation for passing through the door, when again the same sharp cry startled her, and lifting her head suddenly she bumped it against the lintel. The pain of the blow was rather severe.

"What did you do that for?" she exclaimed angrily. "Why did you scream out like that? I——" But she said no more. The cry was repeated, and this time it did its work effectually, for Olive awoke. Awoke—was it waking?—to find herself all in the dark, stiff and cold, and her head aching with the bump she had given it against the old tree-trunk, while farther off now she heard the same shrill hoot or cry of some early astir night-bird, which had sounded before in her dreams.

"Oh dear! oh dear!" she sobbed, "what shall I do? Where am I? How can I ever find my way in the dark? I believe it was all a trick of those nasty blue dwarfs. I don't believe I *was* dreaming. They must be spiteful goblins. I wish I had not gone with them to see their village." And so for some minutes, half asleep and half awake, Olive stayed crouching by the tree, which seemed her only protector. But by degrees, as her senses—her common sense particularly—came back to her, she began to realize that it was worse than useless to sit there crying. Dark as it was, she must try to

find her way back to the little inn, where, doubtless,
Auntie and the others were in the greatest distress
about her, the thought of which nearly made
her burst out crying again; and poor Olive
stumbled up to her feet as best she could, fortunately not forgetting to feel for her book and parasol which were lying beside her, and slowly and
tremblingly made her way on a few steps, hoping
that perhaps if she could manage to get out of the
shadow of the trees it might not be quite so dark
farther on. She was not altogether disappointed.
It certainly grew a very little less black, but that it
was a very dark night there was no denying. And, indeed, thought it had not been dark, she would have
had the greatest difficulty in finding her way out
of the wood, into which she had so thoughtlessly pen-
etrated. Terrifying thoughts, too, began to crowd
into her mind, though, as I think I have shown
you, she was not at all a timid child. But a forest
on a dark night, and so far away from everywhere
—it was enough to shake her nerves. She hoped
and trusted there was no fear of wolves in summer-
time; but bears!—ah! as to bears there was no
telling. Even the hooting cries of the birds which
she now and again heard in the distance frightened
her, and she felt that a bat flapping against her
would send her nearly out of her mind. And after a

while she began to lose heart—it was not quite so
dark, but she had not the very least idea where
she was going. She kept bumping and knocking
herself against the trunks; she was evidently not in
a path, but wandering farther and farther among
the forest trees. That was about all she could feel
sure of, and after two or three more vain efforts
Olive fairly gave up, and, sinking down on the
ground, again burst into tears.

"If I but had a mariner's compass," she thought,
her fancy wandering off to all the stories of lost
people she had ever heard of. Then she further re-
flected that a compass would do her very little
good if it was too dark to see it, and still more as
she had not the slightest idea whether her road lay
north, south. east, or west. "If the stars were
out!" was her next idea; but then, I am ashamed
to say, Olive's ideas of astronomy were limited.
She could have perhaps recognized the Plough and
the Pole star, but she could not remember which
way they pointed. Besides, she did not feel quite
sure that in Thuringen one would see the same
stars as in England or Paris; and, after all, as
there were none visible, it was no good puzzling
about it, only if they *had* been there it would not
have seemed so lonely. Suddenly—what was that
in the distance? A light, a tiny light, bobbing in

and out of sight among the trees? Could it be a
star come out of its way to take pity on her?
Much more likely a Will-o'-the-wisp; for she did not
stop to reflect that a dry pine forest in summer-
time is not one of Will-o'-the-wisp's favorite play-
grounds. It was a light, as to that there was no
doubt, and it was coming nearer. Whether she
was more frightened or glad Olive scarcely knew.
Still, almost anything was better than to sit there
to be eaten up by bears, or to die of starvation;
and she eagerly watched the light now steadily
approaching her, till it came near enough for her
to see that it was a lantern carried by some person
not high above the ground. A boy perhaps; could
it be—oh, joyful thought!—could it be Rex? But
no; even if they were all looking for her it was not
likely that they would let Rex be running about
alone to get lost too. Still, it must *be* a boy, and
without waiting to think more Olive called out—

"Oh, please come and help me! I'm lost in the
wood!" she cried, thinking nothing of German or
anything but her sore distress.

The lantern moved about undecidedly for a
moment or two, then the light flashed towards
her and came still nearer.

"*Ach Gott!*" exclaimed an unfamiliar voice, and
Olive, peering forward, thought for half a second

she was again dreaming. He was not, certainly, dressed in blue, and he was a good deal taller than up to her knee; but still he was—there was no doubt about it—he was a dwarf! And another gaze at his queer little figure and bright sparkling eyes told Olive that it was the very same little man who had smiled at Rex and her when he saw them leaning out of the inn window that very afternoon.

She didn't feel frightened; he looked so good-natured and so sorry for her. And somehow Olive's faith in the possible existence of a nation of dwarfs had received a shock; she was much more inclined to take things prosaically but it was very difficult to explain matters. I think the dwarf at the first moment was more inclined to take *her* for something supernatural than she was now to imagine him a brownie or a gnome. For she was a pretty little girl, with a mass of golden fair hair and English blue eyes; and with her hat half fallen off, and her cheeks flushed, she might have sat for a picture of a fairy who had strayed from her home.

Her German seemed all to go out of her head. But she managed to remember the name of the village where they had been that afternoon, and a sudden recollection seemed to come over the dwarf. He poured out a flood of words and exclamations, amidst which all that Olive could understand was

the name of the village and the words "*verirrt*,"
"*armes Kind*," which she knew meant "lost" and
"poor child." Then he went on to tell that he too
was on his way from the same village to somewhere; that he came by the woods, because it was
shorter, and lifting high his lantern, gave Olive to
understand that he could now show her the way.

So off she set under his guidance, and, only
fancy! a walk of not more than ten minutes
brought them to the little inn! Olive's wanderings
and straying had, after all, drawn her very near
her friends if she had known it. Poor Auntie and
Rex were running about in front of the house in
great distress, Uncle and the landlord and the
coachman had set off with lanterns, and the land-
lady was trying to persuade Auntie that there was
not *really* anything to be afraid of; neither bears,
nor wolves, nor evilly-disposed people about; the
little young lady had, doubtless, fallen asleep in
the wood with the heat and fatigue of the day;
which, as you know, was a very good guess, though
the landlady little imagined what queer places and
people Olive had been visiting in her sleep.

The dwarf was a well-known person thereabouts,
and a very harmless, kindly little man. A present
of a couple of marks sent him off to his cottage
near by very happy indeed, and when Uncle re-

turned a few minutes later to see if the wanderer
had been heard of, you can imagine how thankful
he was to find her. It was not so *very* late after
all, not above half-past ten o'clock, but a thunder-
storm which came on not long after explained the
unusual darkness of the cloud-covered sky.

"*What* a good thing you were safe before the
storm came on!" said Auntie, with a shudder at
the thought of the dangers her darling had escaped.
"I will take care never again to carry my jokes
too far," she resolved, when Olive had confided to
her the real motive of her wanderings in the wood.
And Olive, for her part, decided that she would be
content with fairies and dwarfs in books and fancy,
without trying to find them in reality.

"Though all the same," she said to herself, "I
should have liked to taste the roast fir-cones.
They did smell so good!" "And, Auntie," she
said aloud, "were you singing in the wood on your
way home with Uncle and Rex?"

"Yes," said Auntie, "they begged me to sing
'Home, sweet Home.' Why do you ask me?"

Olive explained. "So it was *your* voice I heard
when I thought it was the dwarfs," she said, smil-
ing.

And Auntie gave her still another kiss.

THE END

THE FLOWERS' WORK

"See, mother! I've finished my bouquet. Isn't it beautiful? More so, I think, than those made by the florist which he asked two dollars for, and this has cost me but seventy-five cents."

"Yes, yes, it is very pretty. But, dear me, child, I cannot help thinking how illy we can spare so much for such a very useless thing. Almost as much as you can make in a day it has cost."

"Don't say *useless*, mother. It will express to Edward our appreciation of his exertions and their result, and our regards. How he has struggled to obtain a profession! I only wish I could cover the platform with bouquets, baskets and wreaths tonight, when he receives his diploma."

"Well, well; if it will do any good, I shall not mind the expense. But, child, he will know it is from you, and men don't care for such things coming from home folks. Now, if it was from any other young lady, I expect he'd be mightily pleased."

"Oh, mother, I don't think so. Edward will think as much of it, coming from his sister-in-law, as from any other girl. And it will please Kate, too. If *we* do not think enough of him to send him bouquets, who else could? Rest easy, mother, dear; I feel

3

quite sure my bouquet will do much good," answered Annie, putting her bouquet in a glass of water.

She left the room to make her simple toilet for the evening.

Mrs. Grey had been widowed when her two little girls were in their infancy. It had been a hard struggle for the mother to raise her children. Constant toil, privation and anxiety had worn heavily on her naturally delicate constitution, until she had become a confirmed invalid. But there was no longer a necessity for her toiling. Katy, the elder daughter, was married; and Annie, a loving, devoted girl, could now return the mother's long and loving care. By her needle she obtained a support for herself and mother.

Katy's husband held a position under the government, receiving a small compensation, only sufficient for the necessities of the present, and of very uncertain continuance. He was ambitious of doing better than this for himself, as well as his family. So he employed every spare hour in studying medicine, and it was the night that he was to receive his diploma that my little story begins.

The exercises of the evening were concluded. Edward Roberts came down the aisle to where his wife and Annie were seated, bearing his flowers — an elegant basket, tastefully arranged, and a beautiful bouquet. But it needed only a quick glance for Annie to see it was not *her* bouquet. Although the flowers were fragrant and rare, they were not so carefully selected or well chosen. Hers expressed not alone her affection and appreciation, but *his* energy, perseverance and success.

"Why, where is my bouquet? I do not see it," asked Annie, a look of disappointment on her usually bright face.

"Yours? I do not know. Did you send me one?" returned her brother-in-law.

"Indeed I did. And such a beauty, too! It is too bad! I suppose it is the result of the stupidity of the young man in whose hands I placed it. I told him plain enough it was for you, and your name, with mine, was on the card," answered Annie, really very much provoked.

"Well, do not fret, little sister; I am just as much obliged; and perchance some poor fellow not so fortunate as I may have received it," answered Edward Roberts.

"Don't, for pity's sake, let mother know of the mistake, or whatever it is, that has robbed you of your bouquet. She will fret dreadfully about it," said Annie.

All that night, until she was lost in sleep, did she constantly repeat:

"I wonder who has got it?"

She had failed to observe on the list of graduates the name of *Edgar Roberts*, from Ohio, or she might have had an idea into whose hands her bouquet had fallen. Her brother Edward, immediately on hearing Annie's exclamation, thought how the mistake had occurred, and was really glad that it was as it was; for the young man whose name was so nearly like his own was a stranger in the city, and Edward had noticed his receiving *one* bouquet only, which of course was the missing one, and Annie's.

Edgar Roberts sat in his room that night, after his

return from the distribution of diplomas, holding in his hand Annie's bouquet, and on the table beside him was a floral dictionary. An expression of gratification was on his pleasant face, and, as again and again his eyes turned from the flowers to seek their interpreter, his lips were wreathed with smiles, and he murmured low:

"Annie Grey! Sweet Annie Grey! I never dreamed of any one in this place knowing or caring enough for me to send such a tribute. How carefully these flowers are chosen! What a charming, appreciative little girl she is! Pretty, I know, of course. I wonder how she came to send me this? How shall I find her? Find her I must, and know her."

And Edgar Roberts fell asleep to dream of Annie Grey, and awoke in the morning whispering the last words of the night before:

"Sweet Annie Grey!"

During the day he found it quite impossible to fix his mind on his work; mind and heart were both occupied with thoughts of Annie Grey. And so it continued to be until Edgar Roberts was really in love with a girl he knew not, nor had ever seen. To find her was his fixed determination. But how delicately he must go about it. He could not make inquiry among his gentlemen acquaintances without speculations arising, and a name sacred to him then, passed from one to another, lightly spoken, perhaps. Then he bethought himself of the city directory; he would consult that. And so doing he found Greys innumerable — some in elegant, spacious dwellings, some in the business thoroughfares of the place. The young ladies of the first mentioned, he thought, living in

fashionable life, surrounded by many admirers, would
scarcely think of bestowing any token of regard
or appreciation on a poor unknown student. The
next would have but little time to devote to such
things; and time and thought were both spent in the
arrangement of his bouquet. Among the long list of
Greys he found one that attracted him more than
all the others — a widow, living in a quiet part of
the city, quite near his daily route. So he sought and
found the place and exact number. Fortune favored
him. Standing at the door of a neat little frame cottage he beheld a young girl talking with two little
children. She was not the blue-eyed, golden-haired
girl of his dreams, but a sweet, earnest dove-eyed
darling. And what care he, whether her eyes were
blue or brown, if her name were only Annie? Oh,
how could he find out that?

She was bidding the little ones "good-bye." They
were off from her, on the sidewalk, when the elder
child — a bright, laughing boy of five — sang out,
kissing his little dimpled hand:

"Good-bye, Annie, darling!"

Edgar Roberts felt as if he would like to clasp the
little fellow to the heart he had relieved of all anxiety.
No longer a doubt was in his mind. He had found
his Annie Grey.

From that afternoon, twice every day he passed the
cottage of the widow Grey, frequently seeing sweet
Annie. This, however, was his only reward. She
never seemed at all conscious of his presence. Often
her eyes would glance carelessly toward him. Oftener
they were never raised from her work. Sewing by
the window, she always was.

What next? How to proceed, on his fixed determination of winning her, if possible?

Another bright thought. He felt pretty sure she attended church somewhere; perhaps had a class in the Sabbath school. So the next Sunday morning, at an early hour, he was commanding a view of Annie's home. When the school bells commenced to ring, he grew very anxious. A few moments, and the door opened and the object of his thoughts stepped forth. How beautiful she looked in her pretty white suit! Now Edgar felt his cause was in the ascendancy. Some distance behind, and on the other side of the street, he followed, ever keeping her in view until he saw her enter a not far distant church. Every Sunday after found him an attentive listener to the Rev. Mr. Ashton, who soon became aware of the presence of the young gentleman so regularly, and apparently so much interested in the services. So the good man sought an opportunity to speak to Edgar, and urge his accepting a charge in the Sabbath school. We can imagine Edgar needed no great urging on that subject; so, frequently, he stood near his Annie. In the library, while selecting books for their pupils, once or twice they had met, and he had handed to her the volume for which her hand was raised. Of course a smile and bow of acknowledgment and thanks rewarded him.

Edgar was growing happier, and more confident of final success every week, when an event came which promised a speedy removal of all difficulty in his path. The school was going to have a picnic. Then and there he would certainly have an introduction to Annie, and after spending a whole day with her, he would accompany her home and win the privilege of calling often.

The day of the picnic dawned brightly, and the happy party gathered on the deck of the steamer. The first person who met Edgar Roberts' eye was his fellow-student, Edward Roberts. Standing beside him were two ladies and some children. When Edgar hastened up to speak to his friend, the ladies turned, and Edward presented:

"My wife; my sister, Miss Grey."

Edgar Roberts could scarcely suppress an exclamation of joy and surprise. His looks fully expressed how delighted he was.

Three months had he been striving for this, which, if he had only known it, could have been obtained so easily through his friend and her brother. But what was so difficult to win was the more highly prized. What a happy day it was!

Annie was all he had believed her — charming in every way. Edgar made a confidant of his friend; told him what Edward well knew before, but was wise enough not to explain the mistake — of his hopes and fears; and won from the prudent brother the promise to help him all he could.

Accompanying Annie home that evening, and gaining her permission for him to call again, Edgar lost no time in doing so, and often repeated the call.

Perhaps Annie thought him very fast in his wooing, and precipitate in declaring his love, when, after only a fortnight visiting her, he said:

"Annie, do you like me well enough, and trust in me sufficiently, to allow me to ask your mother to call me her son?"

Either so happy or so surprised was Annie, that she could not speak just then. But roses crowded over her fair face, and she did not try to withdraw the hand he had clasped.

"Say, Annie, love," he whispered. She raised her eyes to his with such a strange, surprised look in them, that he laughed and said:

"You think I am very hasty, Annie. You don't know how long I've loved you, and have waited for this hour."

"Long!—two weeks," she said.

"Why, Annie, darling, it is over three months since I've been able to think of anything save Annie Grey— ever since the night I received my diploma, and your sweet, encouraging bouquet. Since that night I've known and loved you. And how I've worked for this hour!"

And then he told her how it was. And when he had finished, she looked at him, her eyes dancing merrily, and though she tried hard to keep the little rosebud of a mouth demurely shut, it was no use — it would open and let escape a rippling laugh, as she said:

"And this is the work my bouquet went about, is it? This is the good it has done me—" She hesitated; the roses deepened their color as she continued "And you—"

"Yes, Annie, it has done much good to me, and I hope to you too."

"But, Edgar—" it was the first time she had called him thus, and how happy it made him—"I must tell you the truth — I never sent you a bouquet!"

"No! oh, do not say so. Can there be another such Annie Grey?"

"No; I am the one who sent the bouquet; but, Edgar, you received it through a mistake. It was intended for my brother-in-law, Edward!"

"Stop, Annie, a moment—Are you sorry that mistake was made? Do you regret it?" said Edgar, his voice filled with emotion.

"No indeed. I am very glad you received it instead," Annie ingenuously replied; adding quickly, "But, please, do not tell Edward I said so."

"No, no; I will not tell him that you care a little more for *Edgar* than *Edward*. Is that it? May I think so, Annie?"

She nodded her head, and he caught her to his heart, whispering:

"Mine at last. My Annie, darling! What a blessed mistake it was! May I go to your mother, Annie?"

"Yes; and I'll go with you, Edgar, and hear if she will admit those flowers did any good. She thought it a useless expenditure."

The widow Grey had become very much attached to the kind, attentive young man, and when he came with Annie, and asked her blessing on their love, she gave it willingly; and after hearing all about the way it happened, she said:

"Never did flowers such a good work before. They carried Edgar to church, made a Christian of him, and won for Annie a good, devoted husband, and for me an affectionate son."

THE END.